Clearing her throat, she said, 'We ought to talk about practicalities.'

'I'll come and pick you up, and we'll go back to Montluce together. Once we're there, you won't have to do much,' Philippe said. 'Hang around with me. Convince my great-aunt that you adore me. Hold my hand like this. The usual stuff.'

'Where—?' She stopped, mortified by how high her voice sounded, and coughed. 'Where will I stay?' That was better—huskier, almost normal.

'With me,' said Philippe. His eyes met hers. He clearly knew exactly the way her mind was going. 'Of course we'll have to sleep together,' he said.

Caro managed to tug her hand away at last. It was all very well for Philippe to sound coolly amused about the whole business, but he must have slept with millions of beautiful women.

Philippe naked… Caro's mind veered off track momentarily, to imagine him pulling off his shirt with a grin. The power and the grace and the sheer, sinful sexiness of him.

Her cheeks burned at the thought. She *really* didn't want her imagination to start running wild like that. No, there would be no undressing going on—under any circumstances.

ORDINARY GIRL IN A TIARA

BY
JESSICA HART

First published in Great Britain 2011
by Mills & Boon, an imprint of Harlequin (UK) Limited,
Eton House, 18-24 Paradise Road, Richmond, Surrey TW9 1SR

© Jessica Hart 2011

ISBN: 978 0 263 22033 9

Harlequin (UK) policy is to use papers that are natural, renewable and recyclable products and made from wood grown in sustainable forests. The logging and manufacturing process conform to the legal environmental regulations of the country of origin.

Printed and bound in Great Britain
by CPI Antony Rowe, Chippenham, Wiltshire

Jessica Hart was born in West Africa, and has suffered from itchy feet ever since—travelling and working around the world in a wide variety of interesting but very lowly jobs, all of which have provided inspiration on which to draw when it comes to the settings and plots of her stories. Now she lives a rather more settled existence in York, where she has been able to pursue her interest in history, although she still yearns sometimes for wider horizons. If you'd like to know more about Jessica, visit her website: www.jessicahart.co.uk

CHAPTER ONE

To: caro.cartwright@u2.com
From: charlotte@palaisdemontvivennes.net
Subject: Internet dating
Dear Caro
What a shame about the deli folding. I know you loved that job. You must be really fed up, but your email about the personality test on that internet dating site really made me laugh—good to know you haven't lost your sense of humour in spite of everything that skunk George did to you! All I can say is that compared to Grandmère's matchmaking schemes, internet dating sounds the way to go. Perhaps we should swap lives??!
Lotty
xxxxxxxxxxxxxxxxxx

To: charlotte@palaisdemontvivennes.net
From: caro.cartwright@u2.com
Subject: Swapping places
What a brilliant idea, Lotty! My life is a giddy whirl at the moment, what with temping at a local insurance company and trying to write profile for new dating site (personality test results too depressing on other one) but if you'd like to try it, you're more than welcome! Of course,

living your life would be tough for me—living in a palace, having (admittedly terrifying) grandmother introducing me to suitable princes and so on—but for you, Lotty, anything! Just let me know where and when and I'll have a stab at being a princess for a change...ooh, that's just given me an idea for my new profile. Who says fantasy isn't good for you???

Yours unregally

Caro XXX

> PRINCESS SEEKS FROG: Curvaceous, fun-loving brunette, 28, looking for that special guy for good times out and in.

'What do you think?' Caro read out her opening line to Stella, who was lying on the sofa and flicking through a copy of *Glitz*.

Stella looked up from the magazine, her expression dubious. 'It doesn't make sense. Princess seeks frog? What's that supposed to mean?'

'It means I'm looking for an ordinary guy, not a Prince Charming in disguise. I thought it was obvious,' said Caro, disappointed.

'No ordinary guy would ever work that out, I can tell you that much,' said Stella. She went back to flicking. 'You don't want to be cryptic or clever. Men hate that.'

'It's all so difficult.' Caro deleted the offending words on the screen, and chewed her bottom lip. 'What about the curvaceous bit? I'm worried it might make me sound fat, but there's not much point in meeting someone who's looking for a slender goddess, is there? He'd just run away screaming the moment he laid eyes on me. Besides, I want to be honest.'

'If you're going to be honest, you'd better take out "fun-loving",' Stella offered. 'It makes it sound as if you're up for anything.'

'That's the whole point. I'm changing. Being sensible didn't get me anywhere with George, so I'm going to be a good time girl from now on.'

She would be like Melanie, all giggles and low cut tops and flirty looks. Melanie, who had sashayed into George's office and knocked Caro's steady, sensible fiancé off his feet.

'I can't say what I'm really like or no one will want to go out with me,' she added glumly.

'Rubbish,' said Stella. 'Say you're kind and generous and a brilliant cook—*that* would be honest.'

'Guys don't want kind, even if they say they do,' Caro said bitterly, remembering George. 'They want sexy and fun-loving.'

'Hmm, well, if you want to be sexy, you'd better do something about your clothes,' said Stella, lowering *Glitz* so that she could inspect her friend's outfit with a critical eye. 'I know you're into the vintage look, but a *crochet top*?'

'It's an original from the Seventies.'

'And it was vile then, too.'

Caro made a face at her. With the top she was wearing a tartan miniskirt from the nineteen-sixties and bright red pumps. She was the first to admit that she couldn't *always* carry off the vintage look successfully, but she had been pleased with this particular outfit until Stella had started shaking her head.

Still, there was no point in arguing. She went back to her profile. 'OK, what about *Keen cook seeks fellow foodie*?'

'You'll just get some guy who wants to tie you to the stove and expect you to have his dinner ready the moment he comes through the door. You've already done that for George, and look where that got you.' Stella caught the flash of pain on her friend's face and her voice softened. 'I know how miserable you've been, Caro, but honestly, you're well out of it. George wasn't the right man for you.'

'I know.' Caro caught herself sighing and squared her shoulders. 'It's OK, Stella. I'm fine now. I'm moving on, aren't I?'

Pressing the backspace key with one finger, she deleted the last sentence. 'It's just so depressing having to sign up to these online dating sites. I don't remember it being this hard before. It's like in the five years I was with George, all the single men round here have disappeared into some kind of Bermuda Triangle!'

'Yeah, it's called marriage,' said Stella. She picked up *Glitz* again and flicked through in search of the page she wanted. 'I don't know why you're looking in Ellerby, though. Why don't you get your friend Lotty to introduce you to some rich, glamorous men who eat in Michelin starred restaurants all the time?'

Caro laughed, remembering Lotty's email. 'I wish! But poor Lotty never gets within spitting distance of an interesting man either. You'd think, being a princess, she'd have a fantastically glamorous time, but her grandmother totally runs her life. Apparently she's trying to fix Lotty up with someone "suitable" right now.' Caro hooked her fingers in the air to emphasise the inverted commas. 'I mean, who wants a man your grandmother approves of? I think I'd rather stick with internet dating!'

'I wouldn't mind if he was anything like the guy Lotty's going out with at the moment,' said Stella. 'I saw a picture of them just a second ago. If he was her grandmother's choice, I'd say she's got good taste and she can fix me up any time!'

'Lotty's actually going out with someone?' Caro swivelled round from the computer and stared at Stella. 'She didn't say that! Who is he?'

'Give me a sec. I'm trying to find that photo of her.' When

the flicking failed, Stella licked her finger and tried turning the pages one by one. 'I can never get over you being friends with a real princess. I wish I'd been to a posh school like yours.'

'You wouldn't have liked it. It was fine if you had a title and your own pony and lots of blonde hair to toss around, but if you were only there because your mum was a teacher and your dad the handyman, they didn't want to know.'

'Lotty wanted to know you,' Stella pointed out, still searching.

'Lotty was different. We started on the same day and we were both the odd ones out, so we stuck together. We were both fat and spotty and had braces, and poor Lotty had a stammer too.'

'She's not fat and spotty now,' said Stella. 'She looked lovely in that picture...ah, here it is!'

Folding back the page, she read out the caption under one of the photographs on the *Party! Party! Party!* page. 'Here we go: *Princess Charlotte of Montluce arriving at the Nightingale Ball—fab dress, by the way—with Prince Philippe.*

'*Philippe, the lost heir to Montluce, has only recently returned to the country,*' she read on. '*The ball was their first public outing as a couple, but behind the scenes friends say they are "inseparable" and royal watchers are expecting them to announce their engagement this summer. Is one of Europe's most eligible bachelors off the market already?*'

'Let me see that!' Caro whipped the magazine out of Stella's hands and frowned down at the shiny page. 'Lotty and *Philippe*? I don't believe it!'

But there was Lotty, looking serene, and there, next to her, was indeed His Serene Highness Prince Philippe Xavier Charles de Montvivennes.

She recognised him instantly. That summer he had been seventeen, just a boy, but with a dark, reckless edge to his glamorous looks that had terrified her at the time. Thirteen years on, he looked taller, broader, but still lean, still dangerous. He had the same coolly arrogant stare for the camera, the same sardonic smile that made Caro feel fifteen again: breathless, awkward, painfully aware that she didn't belong.

Stella sat up excitedly. 'You *know* him?'

'Not really. I spent part of a summer holiday in France with Lotty once, and he was part of a whole crowd that used to hang around the villa. It was just before Dad died and, to be honest, I don't remember much about that time now. I know I felt completely out of place, but I do remember Philippe,' Caro said slowly. 'I was totally intimidated by him.'

She had a picture of Philippe lounging around the spectacular infinity pool, looking utterly cool and faintly disreputable. There had always been some girl wrapped round him, sleek and slender in a minuscule bikini while Caro had skulked in the shade with Lotty, too shy to swim in her dowdy one-piece while they were there.

'He and the others used to go out every night and make trouble,' she told Stella. 'There were always huge rows about it, and one or other of them would be sent home on some private plane in disgrace for a while.'

'God, it sounds so glamorous,' said Stella enviously. 'Did you get to go trouble-making too?'

'Are you kidding?' Caro hooted with laughter. 'Lotty and I would never have had the nerve to go with them. Anyway, I'm quite sure Philippe didn't even realise we were there most of the time. Although, actually, now I think about it, he *was* nice to me when I heard Dad was in hospital,' she remembered. 'He said he was sorry and asked if I wanted to go out with the rest of them that night. I'd forgotten that.'

Caro looked down at the magazine again, trying to fit the angular boy she remembered into the picture of the man. How funny that she should remember that moment of brusque kindness now. She'd been so distressed about her father that she had wiped almost everything else about that time from her mind.

'Did you go?'

'No, I was too worried about Dad and, anyway, I'd have been terrified. They were all wild, that lot. And Philippe was the wildest of them all. He had a terrible reputation then.

'He had this older brother, Etienne, who was supposed to be really nice, and Philippe was the hellraiser everyone shook their heads about. Then Etienne was killed in a freak water-skiing accident, and after that we never heard any more about Philippe. I think Lotty told me he'd cut off all contact with his father and gone off to South America. Nobody knew then that his father would end up as Crown Prince of Montluce, but I'm surprised he hasn't come back before. Probably been too busy hellraising and squandering his trust fund!'

'You've got to admit it sounds more fun than your average blind date in Ellerby,' Stella pointed out. 'You said you wanted to have fun, and he's obviously the kind of guy who knows how to do that. You should get Lotty to fix you up with one of his cool friends.'

Caro rolled her eyes. 'Do you really see me hanging around with the jet set?'

'I see what you mean.' Pursing her lips, Stella studied her friend. 'You'd definitely have to lose the crochet top!'

'Not to mention about six stone,' said Caro.

She tossed the magazine back to Stella. 'Anyway, I can't think of anything worse than going out with someone like Philippe. You'd have to look perfect all the time. And then, when you were doing all those exciting glamorous things, you wouldn't be able to look as if you were enjoying it, because that's not cool. And you'd have to be stick-thin, which would mean you'd never be able to eat. It would be awful!'

'Lotty doesn't look as if she minds,' said Stella with another glance at the photo. 'And I don't blame her!'

'You never know what Lotty's really thinking. She's been trained to always smile, always look as if she's enjoying herself, even if she's bored or sick or fed up. Being a princess doesn't sound any fun to me,' said Caro. 'Lotty's been a good girl all her life, and she's never had the chance to be herself or meet someone who'll bother to get to know her rather than the perfect princess she has to be all the time.'

A faint line between her brows, she turned back to the computer and opened Lotty's last email message. Why hadn't Lotty said anything about Philippe then?

To: charlotte@palaisdemontvivennes.net
From: caro.cartwright@u2.com
Subject: ?????????????
You and Philippe??????????????????????????????????????

Lotty's reply came back the next morning.

To: caro.cartwright@u2.com
From: charlotte@palaisdemontvivennes.net
Subject: Re: ?????????????
Grandmère is up to her old tricks again and this time it's serious. I can't tell you what it's like here. I'm getting desperate!

Caro, remember how you said you'd do anything for me when we joked about swapping lives for a while? Well, I've got an idea to put to you, and I'm hoping you weren't joking about the helping bit! I really need to explain in person, but you know how careful I have to be on the phone here, and I can't leave Montluce just yet. Philippe is in London this week, though, so I've given him your number and he's going to get in touch and explain all about it. If my plan works, it could solve our problems for all of us!

Lxxxxxxxxxxxxxxxxx

Deeply puzzled, Caro read Lotty's message again. What plan, and what did Philippe have to do with it? She couldn't imagine Philippe de Montvivennes solving any of *her* problems, that was for sure. What could he do? Make George dump Melanie and come crawling back to her on his knees? Persuade the bank that the delicatessen where she'd been working hadn't gone bankrupt after all?

And what problems could *he* possibly have? Too much money in his trust fund? Too many gorgeous women hanging round him?

Philippe will explain. A real live prince, heir to the throne of Montluce, was going to ring her, Caro Cartwright. Caro nibbled her thumbnail and tried to imagine the conversation. *Oh, hi, yeah*, she would say casually when he called. *Lotty mentioned you would ring.*

She wished she knew what Lotty had told him about her. Not the truth, she hoped. Philippe would only sneer if he knew just how quiet and ordinary her life was.

Not that she cared what he thought, Caro reminded herself hastily. She loved living in Ellerby. Her dreams were ordinary ones: a place to belong, a husband to love, a job she enjoyed. A kitchen of her own, a family to feed. Was that too much to ask?

But Philippe had always lived in a different stratosphere. How could he know that she had no interest in a luxury yacht or a designer wardrobe or hobnobbing with superstars, or whatever else he'd been doing with himself for the past five years? She wouldn't mind eating in the Michelin starred restaurants, Caro allowed, but otherwise, no, she was happy with her lot—or she would be if George hadn't dumped her for Melanie and the deli owner hadn't gone bankrupt.

No, Philippe would never be able to understand that. So perhaps she shouldn't be casual after all. She could sound preoccupied instead, a high-powered businesswoman, juggling million pound contracts and persistent lovers, with barely a second to deal with a playboy prince. *I'm a bit busy at the moment*, she could say. *Could I call you back in five minutes?*

Caro rather liked the idea of startling Philippe with her transformation from gawky fifteen-year-old to assured woman of the world, but abandoned it eventually. For one thing, Philippe would never remember Lotty's friend, plump and plain in her one-piece black swimsuit, so the startle effect was likely to be limited. And, for another, she was content with her own life and didn't need to pretend to be anything other than what she was, right?

Right.

So why did the thought of talking to him make her so jittery?

She wished he would ring and get it over with, but the phone remained obstinately silent. Caro kept checking it to see if the battery had run out, or the signal disappeared for some reason. When it did ring, she would leap out of her skin and fumble frantically with it in her hands before she could even check who was calling. Invariably it was Stella, calling to discover if Philippe had rung yet, and Caro got quite snappy with her.

Then she was even crosser with herself for being so twitchy. It was only Philippe, for heaven's sake. Yes, he was a prince, but what had he ever done other than go to parties and look cool? She wasn't impressed by him, Caro told herself, and was mortified whenever she caught herself inspecting her reflection or putting on lipstick, as if he would be able to see what she looked like when he called.

Or as if he would care.

In any case, all the jitteriness was quite wasted because Philippe didn't ring at all. By Saturday night, Caro had decided that there must have been a mistake. Lotty had misunderstood, or, more likely, Philippe couldn't be bothered to do what Lotty had asked him to do. Fine, thought Caro grouchily. See if she cared. Lotty would call when she could and in meantime she would get on with her life.

Or, rather, her lack of life.

A summer Saturday, and she had no money to go out and no one to go out with. Caro sighed. She couldn't even have a glass of wine as she and Stella were both on a diet and had banned alcohol from the house. It was all right for Stella, who had gone to see a film, but Caro was badly in need of distraction.

For want of anything better to do, she opened up her laptop and logged on to right4u.com. Her carefully worded profile, together with the most flattering photo she could find—taken before George had dumped her and she was two sizes thinner—had gone live the day before. Perhaps someone had left her a message, she thought hopefully. Prince Philippe might not be prepared to get in touch, but Mr Right might have fallen madly in love with her picture and be out there, longing for her to reply.

Or not.

Caro had two messages. The first turned out to be from a fifty-six-year-old who claimed to be 'young at heart' and boasted of having his own teeth and hair although, after one look at his photo, Caro didn't think either were much to be proud of.

Quickly, she moved onto the next message, which was from a man who hadn't provided a picture but who had chosen Mr

Sexy as his code name. Call her cynical, but she had a feeling that might be something of a misnomer. According to the website, the likelihood of a potential match between them was a mere seven per cent. *I want you to be my soulmate*, Mr Sexy had written. *Ring me and let's begin the rest of our lives right now.*

Caro thought not.

Depressed, she got up and went into the kitchen. She was starving. That was the trouble with diets. You were bored and hungry the whole time. How was a girl supposed to move on with her life when she only had salad for lunch?

In no time at all she found the biscuits Stella had hidden in with the cake tins, and she was on her third and wondering whether she should hope Stella wouldn't notice or eat them all and buy a new packet when the doorbell rang. Biscuit in hand, Caro looked at the clock on wall. Nearly eight o'clock. An odd time for someone to call, at least in Ellerby. Still, whoever it was, they surely had to be more interesting than trawling through her potential matches on right4u.com.

Stuffing the rest of the biscuit into her mouth, Caro opened the door.

There, on the doorstep, stood Prince Philippe Xavier Charles de Montvivennes, looking as darkly, dangerously handsome and as coolly arrogant as he had in the pages of *Glitz* and so bizarrely out of place in the quiet Ellerby backstreet that Caro choked, coughed and sprayed biscuit all over his immaculate dark blue shirt.

Philippe didn't bat an eyelid. Perhaps his smile slipped a little, he put it quickly back in place as he picked a crumb off his shirt. 'Caroline Cartwright?' With those dark good looks, he should have had an accent oozing Mediterranean warmth but, like Lotty, he had been sent to school in England and, when he opened that mouth, the voice that came out was instead cool and impeccably English. As cool as the strange

silver eyes that were so disconcerting against the olive skin
and black hair.

Still spluttering, Caro patted her throat and blinked at him
through watering eyes. 'I'm—' It came out as a croak, and she
coughed and tried again. 'I'm Caro,' she managed at last.

Dear God, thought Philippe, keeping his smile in place with
an effort. *Caro's lovely*, Lotty had said. *She'll be perfect.*

What had Lotty been thinking? There was no way this Caro
could carry off what they had in mind. He'd pictured someone
coolly elegant, like Lotty, but there was nothing cool and
certainly nothing elegant about this girl. Built on Junoesque
lines, she'd opened the door like a slap in the face, and then
spat biscuit all over him. He'd had an impression of lushness,
of untidy warmth. Of dark blue eyes and fierce brows and a
lot of messy brown hair falling out of its clips.

And of a perfectly appalling top made of purple cheesecloth. It might possibly have been fashionable forty years earlier, although it was hard to imagine anyone ever picking it
up and thinking it would look nice on. Caro Cartwright must
get dressed in the dark.

Philippe was tempted to turn on his heel and get Yan to
drive him back to London, but Lotty's face swam into his
mind. She had looked so desperate that day she had come to
see him. She hadn't cried, but something about the set of her
mouth, about the strained look around her eyes had touched
the heart Philippe had spent years hardening.

Caro will help, I know she will, she had said. *This is my
only chance, Philippe. Please say you'll do it.*

So he'd promised, and now he couldn't go back on his
word.

Dammit.

Well, he was here, and now he'd better make the best of
it. Philippe forced warmth into his smile, the one that more
than one woman had told him was irresistible. 'I'm Lotty's

cousin, Ph—' he began, but Caro waved him to silence, still patting her throat.

'I know who you are,' she said squeakily, apparently resisting the smile without any trouble at all. 'What are you doing here?'

Philippe was momentarily nonplussed, which annoyed him. He wasn't used to being taken aback, and he certainly wasn't used to having his presence questioned quite so abruptly. 'Didn't Lotty tell you?'

'She said you would *ring*.'

That was definitely an accusing note in her voice. Philippe looked down his chiselled nose. 'I thought it would be easier to explain face to face,' he said haughtily.

Easier for him, maybe, thought Caro. *He* hadn't been caught unawares with no make-up on and a mouthful of biscuit.

There was something surreal about seeing him standing there, framed against the austere terrace of houses across the road. Ellerby was a quiet northern town on the edge of the moors, while Philippe in his immaculately tailored trousers and the dark blue shirt open at the neck appeared to have stepped straight out of the pages of *Glitz*. He was tall and tanned with that indefinable aura of wealth and glamour, the assurance that took red carpets as its due.

A pampered playboy prince…Caro longed to dismiss him as no more than that, but there was nothing soft about the line of his mouth, or the hard angles of cheek and jaw. Nothing self-indulgent about the lean, hard-muscled body, nothing yielding in those unnervingly light eyes.

Still, no reason for her to go all breathless and silly.

'You should have rung,' she said severely. 'I might have been going out.'

'*Are* you going out?' asked Philippe, and his expression as his gaze swept over her spoke louder than words. Who in

God's name, it seemed to say, would even consider going out in a purple cheesecloth shirt?

Caro lifted her chin. 'As it happens, no.'

'Then perhaps I could come in and tell you what Lotty wants,' he said smoothly. 'Unless you'd like to discuss it on the doorstep?'

Please say you'll help. Caro bit her lip. She had forgotten Lotty for a moment there. 'No, of course not.'

Behind Philippe, a sleek black limousine with tinted windows waited at the kerb, its engine idling. Tinted windows! Curtains would be twitching up and down the street.

No, this wasn't a conversation she wanted to be having in full view of the neighbours. Caro stood back and held the door open, tacitly conceding defeat. 'You'd better come in.'

The hallway was very narrow, and she sucked in her breath to make herself slimmer as Philippe stepped past her. Perhaps that explained why she suddenly felt dizzy and out of breath. It was as if a panther had strolled past her, all sleek, coiled power and dangerous grace. Had Philippe always been that *big*? That solid? That overwhelmingly male?

She gestured him into the sitting room. It was a mess in there, but that was too bad. If he didn't have the courtesy to ring and let her know he was coming, he couldn't expect the red carpet to be rolled out.

Philippe's lips tightened with distaste as he glanced around the room. He couldn't remember ever being anywhere quite so messy before. Tights hung over radiators and there were clothes and shoes and books and God only knew what else in heaps all over the carpet. A laptop stood open on the coffee table, which was equally cluttered with cosmetics, nail polishes, battery chargers, magazines and cups of half drunk coffee.

He should have known as soon as the car drew up outside that Caro wasn't going to be one of Lotty's usual friends, who were all sophisticated and accomplished and perfectly groomed. They lived on family estates or in spacious apartments in the centre of London or Paris or New York, not in poky provincial terraces like this one.

What, in God's name, had Lotty been thinking?

'Would you like some tea?' Caro asked.

Tea? It was eight o'clock in the evening! Who in their right mind drank tea at this hour? Philippe stifled a sigh. He'd need more than tea to get himself through this mess he'd somehow got himself into.

'I don't suppose you've got anything stronger?'

'If I'd known you were coming I would have stocked up on the Krug,' she said sharply. 'As it is, you'll have to make do with herbal tea.'

Philippe liked to think of himself as imperturbable, but he clearly wasn't guarding his expression as well as he normally did, because amusement tugged at the corner of Caroline Cartwright's generous mouth. 'I can offer nettle, gingko, milk thistle...'

The dark blue eyes gleamed. She was making fun of him, Philippe realised.

'Whatever you're having,' he said, irritated by the fact that he sounded stiff and pompous.

He was *never* pompous. He was never stiff either. He was famous for being relaxed, in fact. There was just something about this girl that rubbed him up the wrong way. Philippe felt as if he'd strayed into a different world, where the usual rules didn't apply. He should be at some bar drinking cocktails with a gorgeous woman who knew just how the game should be played, not feeling disgruntled in this tip of a house being offered tea—and herbal tea at that!—by a girl who thought he was *amusing*.

'A mug of dandelion and horny goat weed tea coming up,' she said. 'Sit down, I'll just be a minute.'

Philippe couldn't wait.

With a sigh, he pushed aside the clutter on the sofa and sat down. He'd let Lotty talk him into this, and now he was going to have to go through with it. And it suited him, Philippe remembered. If Caroline Cartwright was half what Lotty said she was, she would be ideal.

She's not pretty, exactly, Lotty had said. *She's more interesting than that.*

Caro certainly wasn't pretty, but she had a mobile face, with a long upper lip and expressive eyes as dark and blue as the ocean. Philippe could see that she might have the potential to be striking if she tidied herself up and put on some decent clothes. Not his type, of course—he liked his women slender and sophisticated, and Caro was neither—but that was all to the good. The whole point was for her to be someone he wouldn't want to get involved with.

And vice versa, of course.

So he was feeling a little more optimistic when Caro came in bearing two mugs of what looked like hot ditchwater.

Philippe eyed his mug dubiously, took a cautious sip and only just refrained from spitting it out.

Caro laughed out loud at his expression. 'Revolting, isn't it?'

'God, how do you drink that stuff?' Philippe grimaced and pushed the mug away. Perhaps he made more of a deal about it than he would normally have done, but he needed the excuse to hide his reaction to her smile. It had caught him unawares, like a step missed in the dark. Her face had lit up, and he'd felt the same dip of the stomach, the same lurch of the heart.

And her laugh...that laugh! Deep and husky and totally unexpected, it was a tangible thing, a seductive caress, the kind that drained all the blood from your head and sent it straight to your groin while it tangled your breathing into knots.

'It's supposed to be good for you,' Caro was saying, examining her own tea without enthusiasm. 'I'm on a diet. No alcohol, no caffeine, no carbohydrates, no dairy products… basically, no anything that I like,' she said glumly.

'It doesn't sound much fun.' Philippe had managed to get his lungs working again, which was a relief. Her laugh had surprised him, that was all, he decided. A momentary aberration. But listen to him now, his voice as steady as a rock. Sort of.

'It isn't.' Caro sighed and blew on her tea.

She had been glad to escape to the kitchen. Philippe's presence seemed to have sucked all the air out of the house. How was it that she had never noticed before how suffocatingly small it was? There was a strange, squeezed feeling inside her, and she fumbled with the mugs, as clumsy and self-conscious as she had been at fifteen.

Philippe's supercilious expression as he looked around the cosy sitting room had stung, Caro admitted, and she had enjoyed his expression when she had offered the tea. Well, they couldn't all spend their lives drinking champagne, and it wouldn't do him any harm to have tea instead for once.

Caro thought about him waiting in the sitting room, looking faintly disgusted and totally out of place. In wealth and looks and glamour, he was so out of her league it was ridiculous. But that was a good thing, she decided, squeezing the teabags with a spoon. It meant there was no point in trying to impress him, even if she had been so inclined. She could just be herself.

'I'm reinventing myself,' she told him now. 'My fiancé left me for someone who's younger and thinner and more fun, and then I lost my job,' she said. 'I had a few months moping around but now I've pulled myself together. At least I'm trying to. No more misery eating. I'm going to get fit, lose weight, change my life, meet a nice man, live happily ever after...you know, realistic, achievable goals like that.'

Philippe raised an eyebrow. 'It's a lot to expect from drinking tea.'

'The tea's a start. I mean, if I can't stick with this, how am I supposed to stick with all the other life-changing stuff?' Caro took a sip to prove her point, but even she couldn't prevent an instinctive wrinkling of the nose. 'But you didn't come here to talk about my diet,' she reminded him. 'You're here about Lotty.'

CHAPTER TWO

'AH, YES,' said Philippe. 'Lotty.'

Caro put down her mug at his tone. 'Is she OK? I had a very cryptic email from her. She said you would explain about some idea she'd had.'

'She's fine,' he said, 'and yes, I am supposed to be explaining, but it's hard to know where to start. Presumably you know something of the situation in Montluce at the moment?'

'Well, I know Lotty's father died last year.'

The sudden death of Crown Prince Amaury had shocked everyone. He had been a gentle man, completely under the thumb of his formidable mother as far as Caro could tell, and Lotty was his only child. She had taken her dead mother's place at his side as soon as she'd left finishing school, and had never put a foot wrong.

Lotty was the perfect princess, always smiling, always beautiful, endlessly shaking hands and sitting through interminable banquets and never, ever looking bored. There were no unguarded comments from Lotty for the press to seize upon, no photos posted on the internet. No wild parties, no unsuitable relationships, not so much as a whiff of scandal.

'Since then,' Philippe said carefully, 'things have been… rather unsettled.'

'Unsettled' was a bit of an understatement, in Caro's opinion. Montluce was one of the last absolute monarchies in Europe, and had been in the iron grip of the Montvivennes family since Charlemagne. Small as it was, the country was rigidly traditional, and the ruling family even more so. Lotty's grandmother, known as the Dowager Blanche, was only the latest in line of those who made the British royal family's attitude to protocol look slapdash.

Since Lotty's father had died, though, the family had been plunged into a soap opera of one dramatic event after another. A car accident and a heart attack had carried off one heir after another, while one of Lotty's cousins, who should have been in line for the crown, had been disinherited and was currently serving time for cocaine smuggling.

Now, what the tabloids loved to refer to as the 'cursed inheritance' had passed against all the odds to Philippe's father, Honoré. In view of the tragic circumstances, his coronation had been a low-key affair, or so Lotty had told Caro. There had been much speculation in the tabloids about Philippe's absence. None of them could have guessed that the current heir to the throne of Montluce would turn up in Ellerby and be sitting in Stella and Caro's sitting room, pointedly not drinking his horny goat weed tea.

'Amaury was always more interested in ancient Greek history than in running the country,' Philippe went on. 'He was happy to leave the day-to-day business of government in his mother's hands. The Dowager Blanche is used to having things her own way, and now all her plans have gone awry. She's not happy,' he added dryly.

'She doesn't approve of your father?' Caro was puzzled. She'd only ever seen photos of Philippe's father, but he looked tailor-made for the part of Crown Prince. She couldn't imagine why Lotty's grandmother would object to him.

'Oh, he's perfect as far as she's concerned. His sense of duty is quite as strong as hers.' There was an edge to Philippe's voice that Caro didn't understand.

'So what's the problem?' she asked. The truth was that she was having trouble focusing. Part of her was taken up with thinking: there's a *prince* on the sofa! Part was trying not to notice that beneath the casual shirt and trousers, his body was taut and lean.

And another part was so hungry that she couldn't concentrate on any of it properly. She could feel her stomach grumbling. Caro wrapped her arms around her waist and willed it to be quiet. How could she follow Philippe's story when she was worried her stomach might let out an embarrassing growl at any minute?

'Can't you guess?' Philippe smiled but the silver eyes were hard.

Caro forced her mind away from her stomach. 'Oh,' she said slowly. '*You're* the problem?'

'Got it in one,' said Philippe. 'The Dowager thinks I'm idle and feckless and irresponsible and has told me so in no uncertain terms.'

The sardonic smile flashed again. 'She's right, of course. Personally, I've never seen the appeal of duty and commitment. The thought that the future of the Montvivennes dynasty rests with me is almost more than my great-aunt can bear,' he added. 'She's decided that the only way to keep me in line and ensure that I'm not a total disaster for the country is to marry me to Lotty.'

'Lotty said that her grandmother was matchmaking,' said Caro, adding, not very tactfully, 'I'm surprised she'd approve of you, though.'

Philippe acknowledged that with a grim smile. 'She doesn't but, from her point of view, it's the only solution,' he said. 'Once shackled to Lotty, I'll settle down, they think. Lotty's bound to be a good influence on me. She's the perfect princess, after all, and there's no doubt it would be popular in the country. Compared to what the people think, what does it matter what Lotty and I feel?' Bitterness crept into his voice. 'We're royal, and we're expected to do our duty and not complain about it.'

'Poor Lotty! It's so unfair the way she never gets to do what she wants to do.'

'Quite,' said Philippe. He was leaning forward, absently turning his unwanted mug of tea on the coffee table. 'With a new Crown Prince in place, she thought that she would have a chance to get away and make a life of her own at last, but of course my father doesn't have a wife, having been careless enough to let his wife run off with another man, and now Lotty's being manoeuvred into being a consort all over again. I'm fond of Lotty, but I don't want to marry her any more than she wants to marry me.'

'But there must be something you can do about it,' Caro protested. 'I know Lotty finds it hard to resist her grand-mother, but surely you can just say no?'

'I have.' As if irritated by his own fiddling, Philippe pushed the mug away once more and sat back. 'But the Dowager doesn't give up that easily. She's always pushing Lotty and I together and leaking stories to the press.'

'It said in *Glitz* that you were inseparable,' remembered Caro and he nodded grimly.

'That's the Dowager's handiwork. She adores that magazine because they're so pro-royalty. And you've got to admit, it's not a bad strategy. Start a rumour, let everyone in the country whip themselves up into wedding fever and wait for Lotty to cave under the pressure. Montlucians love Lotty, and she'll hate feeling that she's disappointing everyone by being selfish, as the Dowager puts it.'

Caro's mouth turned down as she thought about it. It did seem unfair. 'Why don't you go back to South America?' she suggested. 'Surely the Dowager Blanche would give up on the idea of you and Lotty eventually.'

'That's the trouble. I can't.' Restlessly, Philippe got to his feet. He looked as if he wanted to pace, but the room wasn't big enough for that, so he picked his way through the clutter to the bay window and stood staring unseeingly out to where the limousine waited at the kerb.

'It hasn't been announced yet, but my father is ill,' he said, his back to Caro. 'It's cancer.'

'Oh, no.' Caro remembered how desperate she had felt when her own father had been dying, and wished that she had the courage to get up and lay a sympathetic hand on Philippe's shoulder, but there was a rigid quality to his back that warned her against it. 'I'm so sorry,' she said instead.

Philippe turned back to face her. 'His prognosis isn't too bad, in fact, but the press are going to have a field day with the curse of the House of Montvivennes when it comes out.' His face was carefully expressionless.

'Montluce doesn't have specialised facilities, so he's going to Paris for treatment, and he's been told to rest completely for at least six months. So I've been summoned back to stand in for him. Only nominally, as he and the Dowager keep saying, but they're big on keeping up appearances. I'm taking over his commitments from the start of the month.

'I thought about refusing at first. My father and I don't have what you'd call a close relationship,' he went on with an ironic look, 'and I don't see why they need me to shake a few hands or pin on the occasional medal. If I could have some influence on decisions that are made, it would be different, but my father has never forgiven me for not being a perfect son like my older brother. When I suggested that I have some authority, he was so angry that he actually collapsed.'

Philippe sighed. 'I could insist, but he's ill, and he's my father…I don't want to make him even sicker than he is already. In the end, I said I would do as they asked for six months, but on the understanding that I can go back to South

America as soon as he's well again. There's no point in me hanging around with nothing to do but disappoint him that I'm not Etienne.'

So even royal families weren't averse to laying on the emotional blackmail, thought Caro.

'Meanwhile, you're being thrown together with Lotty at every opportunity?' she said.

'Exactly.' He rolled his shoulders as if to relieve the tension there. 'Then, the other day, Lotty and I were on one of our carefully staged "dates" and we came up with a plan.'

'I wondered when we were going to get to the plan,' said Caro. She made herself take another sip of tea. Philippe was right. It was disgusting. 'What is this great idea of Lotty's?'

'It's a simple one. The problem has been that we're both there, and both single. Of course Lotty's grandmother is going to get ideas. But if I go back to Montluce with a girlfriend and am clearly madly in love with her, even the Dowager Blanche would have to stop pushing Lotty and I together for a while.'

Caro could see where this was going. 'And then Lotty can pretend that it's too awkward for her to see you with another woman and tells her grandmother she needs to go away for a while?'

'Exactly,' said Philippe again.

'I suppose it could work.' She turned the idea over in her mind. 'Where do I come into this? Does Lotty want to come and stay here?'

'No,' said Philippe. 'She wants you to be my girlfriend.'

Caro's heart skidded to a stop, did a funny little flip and then lurched into gear again at the realisation that he was joking. 'Right.' She laughed.

Philippe said nothing.

Her smile faltered. 'You can't be serious?'

'Why not?'

'Well, because…you must have a girlfriend.'

'If I had a serious girlfriend, I wouldn't be in this mess,' he said crisply. 'I'm allergic to relationships. When I meet a woman, I'm clear about that, right from the start. No emotions, no expectations. It just gets messy otherwise.'

Caro sighed. 'Commitment issues…I might have guessed! What is it with guys and relationships?'

'What is it with *women* and relationships?' Philippe countered. 'Why do you always have to spoil things by talking about whether we have a relationship or not and, if we do, where it's going? Why can't we just have a good time?'

Balked of the prowling he so clearly wanted to do, Philippe stepped over to the mantelpiece, put his hands in his pockets and glowered down at his shoes as if it was their fault. 'Six months is about as long as I can stand being in Montluce,' he said. 'It's a suffocating place. Formal, stuffy, and so small there's never any chance to get away.'

He lifted his eyes to Caro's. They ought to be dark brown, she thought inconsequentially, not that clear, light grey that was so startling against his dark skin that it sent a tiny shock through her every time she looked into them.

'I'll be leaving the moment my father is better, and I don't want to complicate matters by getting involved with a woman if there's the slightest risk that she'll start taking things seriously. On the other hand, if she gets so much as a whiff that I'm not in fact serious, the Dowager Blanche will have Lotty back in a flash. For me, that would be a pain, as I'd have to go back to fighting off all the matchmaking attempts, but it would be far, far worse for Lotty. She'd lose the first chance she's ever had to do something for herself. And that's why you'd be perfect,' he said to Caro.

'You're Lotty's friend,' he said. 'I could pretend to be in love with you without worrying that you'd get the wrong idea, because you'd know the score from the start. I'm not going to fall in love with you and you don't want to get involved with me.'

'Well, *that's* certainly true,' said Caro, ruffled nonetheless by the brutal truth. *I'm not going to fall in love with you.*

'But you could pretend to love me, couldn't you?'

'I'm not sure I'm that good an actress,' said Caro tartly.

'Not even for Lotty?'

Caro chewed her lip, thinking of her friend. Lotty was so sweet-natured, so stoical, so good at pleasing everyone but herself. Trapped in a gilded cage of duty and responsibility. From the outside, it was a life of luxury and privilege, but Caro knew how desperately her friend longed to be like everyone else, to be ordinary. Lotty couldn't pop down to the shops for a pint of milk. She couldn't go out and get giggly over a bottle of wine. She could never look less than perfect, never be grumpy, never act on impulse, never relax.

She could never have fun without wondering if someone was going to take her picture and splash it all over the tabloids.

I'm getting desperate, Lotty had said in her email.

'No one would ever believe you would go out with someone like me!' Caro said eventually.

Philippe studied her with dispassionate eyes. 'Not at the moment, perhaps, but with a haircut, some make-up, some decent clothes…you might brush up all right.'

Caro tilted her head on one side as she pretended to consider his reply. 'OK, that's one answer,' she allowed. 'Another might be: why wouldn't anyone believe that I could be in love with you? Don't change a thing; you're beautiful as you are.' She smiled sweetly. 'Just a suggestion, of course!'

'See?' said Philippe. 'That's what makes you perfect. I can be honest with you if you're not a real girlfriend.'

'Stop, you're making me feel all warm and fuzzy inside!'

He smiled at that, and went back to sit on the sofa. 'Look,

just think about it seriously for a moment, Caro. You don't need to come for the whole six months. Two or three would probably be enough for Lotty to get away. We'd both know where we were. There would no expectations, nobody needs to get hurt and, at the end of two months or whatever, we could say goodbye with no hard feelings. I stop my great-aunt hassling me about marriage, you get two months away living in a palace—' the glance he sent around the sitting room made it clear what a change *that* would be '—and Lotty gets a chance to escape and have a life of her own for a while.'

He paused. 'Lotty…Lotty needs this, Caro. You know what she's like. Always restrained, always dignified. She wasn't going to cry or anything, but I could tell how desperate she feels. She's been good all her life, and just when it looks as if a door is opening for her at last, the Dowager and my father are trying to slam it closed again.'

'I know, it's so unfair, but—'

'And you did say you wanted to reinvent yourself,' Philippe reminded her.

Caro winced. She had said that. She clutched at her hair, careless of the way it tumbled out of its clip. 'I just don't know… There's so much to consider, and I can't think when I'm hungry like this!' Uncurling her legs, she put her feet on the floor. 'I'm going to get a biscuit,' she announced.

'I've got a better idea,' said Philippe, checking the Rolex on his wrist. 'Why don't I take you out to dinner? We can talk about the practicalities then, and I could do with a proper drink, not that disgusting stuff,' he said with a revolted glance at his tea. 'Where's the best place to eat around here?'

'The Star and Garter at Littendon,' said Caro automatically, perking up at the prospect of dinner. There was the diet, of course, but she couldn't be expected to make life-changing decisions on a salad and three biscuits, could she? Besides, it was Saturday. It was dinner with a prince, or stay at home with herbal tea and Mr Sexy online.

The prince in question might not be quite as charming as in the fairy tales, but it still wasn't what you'd call a hard choice.

'But you'll never get in on a Saturday,' she added as Philippe took out a super-slim phone and slid it open. 'They get booked up months in advance.'

Ignoring her, Philippe put the phone to his ear. 'Why don't you go and get changed?' was all he said. 'I'm not taking you out in that purple thing.'

The *purple thing* happened to be one of Caro's favourites, and she was still bristling as she pulled it over her head. She hoped the Star and Garter refused him a table and told His Obnoxious Highness that he'd have to wait three months like everyone else.

On the other *hand*, she reminded herself, the food was reputed to be fabulous. Way out of her price range, but no doubt peanuts to Philippe. It wouldn't be *so* bad if he got a table after all.

Now, what to wear? The Star and Garter—if that was where they were going, and Caro had the feeling that Philippe usually got what he wanted—deserved one of her best dresses. Caro ran her eye over her collection of vintage clothes and picked a pale blue cocktail dress made of flocked chiffon. Perhaps the neckline was a *little* low, but she loved the way the pleated skirt swished around her legs when she sashayed her hips.

Sucking in her breath to do up the side zip, Caro tugged up the neckline as far as she could and sauntered back downstairs with a confidence she was far from feeling. Philippe was still on the sofa, looking utterly incongruous. Unaware of her arrival—she could have spared herself the sauntering—he

was leaning forward, reading something on the laptop she had
abandoned earlier when she had gone in search of biscuits.

Her laptop! Too late, Caro remembered what she had been
doing when depression had sent her to the kitchen. Shooting
across the room, she banged the laptop closed, narrowing
missing Philippe's fingers.

'What are you *doing*?'

Not at all perturbed, Philippe sat back and looked up at
her.

'You know, I'm not sure Mr Sexy is the right guy for
you.'

'You shouldn't look at other people's computers.' Caro was
mortified that he had witnessed how she had been spending
her Saturday night. She glared at him. 'It's very rude.'

'It was open on the table,' Philippe pointed out, unfazed.
'I couldn't help but see what you'd been doing. It was quite
an eye-opener, I must say. I've never looked at a dating site
before.'

Well, there was a surprise. Young, rich, handsome, a prince,
and he'd never had to resort to internet dating. Incredible,
thought Caro.

'I don't see you finding Mr Right amongst that lot, though,'
he said. 'They're not exactly oozing charisma, are they?'

'They can't all be princes,' snapped Caro, pushing him
out of the way so she could shut the computer down. 'That's
not what I'm looking for either. I just want an ordinary life
with an ordinary guy, which is not something *you'd* be able
to understand.'

Philippe shook his head. 'You know, I don't think you've
been entirely honest in your profile,' he said, nodding at the
computer. 'You didn't say anything about how prickly you
are.'

'You read my profile?'

'Of course,' he said. 'It's called research. If we're going

to be spending time together, I need to know what I'm going to be dealing with. I must say, I don't think that picture does you justice,' he went on.

He eyed Caro's dress, unimpressed. 'You might want to warn any prospective matches about your odd taste in clothes before you meet,' he added with unnecessary provocation. 'What are you wearing *now*?'

'I'll have you know this is one of my best dresses,' she said, too cross with him to care what he thought about her clothes. 'It's an original cocktail dress from the Fifties. I had to save up to buy it online.'

'You mean you handed over money for that?' Philippe unfolded himself from the sofa. 'Extraordinary.'

'I love vintage clothes,' said Caro. She held out the skirts and twirled. 'I wonder who bought this dress when it was new. Did she buy it for a special occasion? Was she excited? Did she meet someone when she was wearing it? A dress like this has a history. I like that.'

Philippe blinked at the swirl of chiffon and the tantalising glimpse of a really excellent pair of legs. The dress was an improvement on the purple cheesecloth, there was no doubt about that, but he wished that she had put on something a little less…eccentric. A little less *provoking*. Only Caroline Cartwright would choose to wear a sixty-year-old dress!

Maybe it did suit those luscious curves, but it still looked odd to Philippe, and he scowled as he sat in the back of the limousine next to Caro. He had decided to ignore—loftily— her fashion faux pas, and was annoyed to discover that the wretched dress kept snagging at his attention anyway. He blamed Caro, who kept tugging surreptitiously at the neckline, which only drew his eyes to the deep cleavage. Or she was crossing those legs so that the chiffon skirt slithered over her thighs. Philippe shifted uneasily, adjusting his seat belt. He was sure he could hear the material whispering silkily against her bare skin. She had twisted up the mass of nut-brown hair and fixed it with a clip so obviously casually shoved in that he expected any moment that it would all tumble free.

It was very distracting.

Caro wasn't supposed to be distracting. She was supposed to be convenient. That was all.

'I can't believe you got a table!' Caro looked as if she couldn't decide whether to be delighted or aggrieved when the limousine pulled up outside the Star and Garter.

'I didn't. Yan did.' Philippe nodded at an impassive giant who sat next to the driver in the front seat.

Caro lowered her voice and leant closer, giving Philippe a whiff of a clean fresh scent. 'Is he your bodyguard?'

'He prefers to be known as my personal protection officer,' said Philippe. 'He's a very handy man to have around, especially when it comes to getting tables.'

'Everyone else has to wait months. I suppose he dropped your title?' she said disapprovingly.

'I'm sure he did. What else is it for?'

'We can go somewhere else if you object to Yan pulling rank,' he said, but Caro shook her head quickly, so that more strands escaped from the clip. She smoothed them from her face.

'I've always wanted to eat here,' she confessed. 'It's horrendously expensive and most people only come for special occasions. I wanted to come with George when we got engaged, but he didn't think it was worth the money.' She sighed a little and the generous mouth curved downwards. 'We had pizza instead.'

To Philippe, who had eaten at some of the world's top restaurants, there was nothing special about the Star and Garter. It was pleasant enough, he allowed, simply decorated with subtle lighting and enough tables for the place to feel lively without being so close together you were forced to listen to anyone else's conversation.

He was used to the way the buzz of conversation paused when he walked into a restaurant, used to ignoring it while the manager came to greet him personally, used to exchanging pleasantries on automatic pilot, but all the time he could *feel* Caro beside him as clearly as if she were touching him. He kept his eyes courteously on the manager, but he didn't need to look at Caro to know that she was looking eagerly around her, practically humming with anticipation, careless of the fact that her fashion sense was fifty years out of date. Her eyes would be bright, that wretched, tantalising hair escaping from its clip.

And then, abruptly, he felt her stiffen and inhale sharply, and he broke off in mid-sentence to glance at her. She was rigid, her face white and frozen. Philippe followed her stricken gaze across the restaurant to where a couple were staring incredulously back at her.

It wasn't his problem, Philippe told himself, but somehow his arm went round Caro and he pulled her into his side in a possessive gesture. 'I hope you're hungry, *chérie*?' he said, trying not to notice how the dress slipped over her skin beneath his hand.

Caro looked blindly up at him. 'Wh…What?'

'Do you want to go straight to the table or would you rather have a drink at the bar first?' He kept a firm hold on her until the blankness faded from her eyes and understanding dawned.

'Oh.' She moistened her lips. 'Let's go to the table.'

'Excellent.' Philippe turned to the manager. 'We'll have a bottle of your best champagne.'

'Certainly, Your Highness.'

Caro was tense within the circle of his arm as they followed the waiter to their table. She didn't look again at the couple, but her lips were pressed tightly together in distress or anger, Philippe couldn't tell.

'All right?' he asked, when the waiter had gone.

'Yes, I…yes.' Caro shook out her napkin and smoothed it on her lap with hands that were not quite steady. 'It was just a shock to see them here.'

'That was your ex, I take it?'

'George, yes, and his new fiancée.' Her voice vibrated with suppressed anger. 'I can't *believe* he brought Melanie here. She doesn't even *eat*! That's how she looks like a stick insect.'

Philippe glanced over at the table. As far as he could see, Melanie was slim and pretty and blonde, but she would look muted next to Caro.

'I wonder if they're celebrating their engagement?' Caro went on, but he was glad to see the colour back in her face. Shock, it seemed, had been superseded by fury. 'Clearly, Melanie's too good for *pizza*!' She practically spat out the word.

'Maybe she'll wish that they'd gone for pizza instead now that you've arrived,' said Philippe, picking up the menu. 'It can't be much fun trying to celebrate your engagement when your fiancé's ex is on the other side of the room and he can't take his eyes off her.'

'Oh, he's not looking at *me*,' said Caro bitterly. 'He's looking at *you* and wondering what on earth a guy like you is doing with a boring frump like me!'

Philippe's dark brows shot up. 'Boring? *You?*'

His surprise was some consolation, Caro supposed. She opened the menu and pretended to read it, but the words were a blur and all she saw instead was George's face the day he'd told her it was over. He'd waited until she came back from the supermarket, and told her while she was unpacking the bags. Now Caro couldn't look at a carton of orange juice without feeling queasy.

'George thinks I'm boring.' She pressed her lips together against the jab of memory. 'He always said that he wanted to marry someone like me, but then he fell in love with Melanie because she was sexy and fun and everything I'm not, apparently.'

Turning a page unseeingly, she went on, 'There's a certain irony in that. I spent five years being careful and dressing conventionally, and deliberately *not* being fun or obvious, just so that I would fit into his world. I'd have done anything for him.'

Whenever she thought about how much she had loved George, her voice would crack like that. It was mortifying because she was over him now. Pretty much.

'Lotty said you'd been engaged, but that it was over,' Philippe said in that cool, couldn't-give-a-damn voice. 'It's one of the reasons she thought you might like to come to Montluce. A chance to get away for a while.'

'It *would* be nice.' Caro hadn't thought of that aspect of things before. She'd been too busy thinking what it would be like to spend two months with Philippe, who was sitting opposite her looking remote and gorgeous and totally out of reach in spite of being only a matter of inches away.

'Ellerby's a small town,' she said, 'and I spend a lot of time dreading that I'm going to bump into George, like just now.'

Although this time it hadn't been so bad, after all, she realised. There'd been that horrible moment when she'd seen George there with Melanie, and she'd been gripped by that old mixture of misery and rage and humiliation. They were a cosy twosome and she was left alone…and then, suddenly, she hadn't been on her own. Philippe had put his arm around her and made it look as if they were a couple, and she'd seen the astonishment flash in George's face.

Caro looked at Philippe. The dark brows were drawn together as he studied the menu and, with those piercing eyes shielded for once, she could let her gaze travel down his straight nose to the cool set of his mouth, where it snagged in spite of her efforts to tear her eyes away. Looking at it made her feel quite…funny.

He hadn't hesitated to step in and rescue her, while she had been floundering.

'Thank you for earlier,' she said.

'Earlier?'

'You know, making George think we were a couple.' He'd been so quick, seeing instantly what was needed, before she'd even thought about how to react. 'They always see me looking lonely and miserable and pathetic,' she said, laying down the menu so that he could see how grateful she was. 'I don't look like that when I'm with you.'

CHAPTER THREE

'ARE you still in love with him?' Philippe asked and then looked as if the question had caught him unawares. 'I mean, it would be difficult for you to act as my girlfriend if you were,' he added.

'No.' She didn't sound quite as sure as she should have done, Caro realised. 'No,' she said again. 'I adored George. When he broke off our engagement, it broke my heart. For a long time I told myself that I wanted him back, that I still loved him, but now…now I think maybe I love the idea of him more than the reality.'

She saw Philippe flick a brief, uncomprehending glance at George. No, he wouldn't understand.

'I know he's not particularly good-looking or glamorous, but he was everything I've ever wanted. He belongs.'

Philippe looked mystified.

'I never belonged anywhere,' she tried to explain. 'My dad was a mechanical engineer, and when I was small we moved around from project to project overseas. Then he got ill, and we moved to St Wulfrida's.'

'That was Lotty's school,' he remembered, and Caro nodded.

'That's where we met. My mother got a teaching post there, Dad applied to be the handyman so they could be together, and I got a free education as part of the deal. Except I was never going to belong in a school like that, where all the other girls had titles or triple-barrelled names. I wasn't nearly posh enough for them. Lotty was my only friend, and I wouldn't have got through it without her.'

'Funny,' said Philippe, 'that's what she said about you.'

Caro smiled. 'We got each other through, I think. Neither of us could wait to leave. St Wulfrida's doesn't exactly excel in academic achievement, so after GCSEs Lotty went to finishing school, and I went to the local college to do A levels. I thought that would be better, but of course I didn't fit in there either. I was *too* posh for them!'

'What's the big deal about belonging, anyway?' asked Philippe. 'You're lucky. You can go wherever you like, do what you like. That's what most of us want.'

'I don't,' said Caro. 'Dad died when I was fifteen, and my mother five years later, so I don't have any family left.'

She smiled wistfully. 'I suppose I've been looking for a home ever since. When I came to Ellerby and met George, I really thought I'd found a place to belong at last,' she went on. 'George's family have been here for generations. He's the third generation of solicitors, and he's *part* of Ellerby.' Caro searched her mind for an example. 'He's on the committee at the golf club.'

Philippe raised his brows.

'I know,' she said, even though he hadn't said a word, 'it doesn't sound very exciting. But being with George made me feel safe. He had a house, and it felt like being part of the community. I think that's what I miss more than anything else.'

The wine waiter arrived with the bottle of champagne just then, and they went through the whole palaver of showing Philippe the label, opening the bottle with a flourish, pouring the glasses.

Caro concentrated on the menu while all that was going on, a little embarrassed by how much she'd blurted out to

Philippe. He was surprisingly easy to talk to, she realised. Perhaps it was because he so clearly didn't care. Or maybe it was knowing that he was so far out of her league she didn't even need to try and impress him with her coolness or her success. She wasn't here to be clever or witty or interesting. It didn't matter what he thought of George, or of her.

The realisation was strangely exhilarating.

When they'd ordered, Philippe picked up his glass and chinked it against hers. 'Shall we drink to our plan?'

Anything for you, Lotty, she had said once. Still in the grip of that odd sense of liberation, Caro touched his glass back with the air of one making an irrevocable decision. 'To our plan,' she agreed. 'And to Lotty's escape.'

Philippe sat back in his chair and eyed her thoughtfully across the table. 'You're good friends, aren't you?'

'Lotty was wonderful to me when my father died.' Caro turned the stem of her champagne glass between her thumb and fingers. 'He'd been ill for months, and there was no question of us going on holiday, so Lotty asked me if I wanted to spend part of the summer with her, in her family villa in the south of France.'

She lifted her eyes and met Philippe's cool ones. 'You were there.'

'Lotty said that we'd met once,' he said. 'I vaguely remember that she had a friend who was around and then suddenly gone. Was that you?'

'Yes. I hung around with Lotty until my mother rang to say that Dad had had a relapse and was in hospital again. She said there was nothing I could do, and that I should stay in France and enjoy myself. She said that was what Dad wanted, but I couldn't bear it. I was desperate to see him.'

The glass winked in the candlelight as Caro turned it round, round, round.

'I didn't have any money, and Mum was too worried

about Dad to think of changing my ticket,' she went on after a moment. 'Lotty was only fifteen too, and she was so shy that she still stammered when she was anxious, but she didn't even hesitate. She knew I needed to go home. She talked to people she would normally be too nervous to talk to, and she sorted everything out for me. She made sure I was booked onto a flight the next day. I've no idea how she did it, but she arranged for someone to pick me up at the airport in London and take me straight to the hospital.

'Dad died the next day.' Caro swallowed. Even after all that time, the thought of her beloved father made her throat tight. 'If it hadn't been for Lotty, I'd never have seen him again.' She lifted her eyes to Philippe's again. 'I'll always be grateful to her for that. I've often wished there was something I could do for her in return, and now I can. If spending two months pretending to be in love with you helps her escape, even if just for a little while, then I'll do that.'

'It must have been a hard time for you,' said Philippe after a moment. 'I know how I felt when my brother died. I wanted everything to just…stop. And I wasn't a child, like you.'

He set his glass carefully on the table. 'Lotty was good to me then, too. Everyone understood how tragic it was for my father to lose his perfect son, but Lotty was the only one who thought about what it might be like for me to lose a brother. She's a very special person,' he said. 'She deserves a chance to live life on her own terms for a change. I know this is a mad plan,' he went on, deliberately lightening the tone, 'but it's worth a shot, don't you think?'

'I do.' Caro was happy to follow his lead. 'If nothing else, it will convince George and Melanie that I've moved on to much bigger and better things!'

She shot George a victorious look, but Philippe shook his head. 'Stop that,' he said.

'Stop what?'

'Stop looking at him.' He tutted. 'When I take a girl out to dinner, I don't expect her to spend her whole time thinking about another man!'

'I'm not!'

'You're supposed to be thinking about *me*,' said Philippe, ignoring her protest. 'George is never going to believe we're having a wild and passionate affair if he sees you sneaking glances at him.'

'He's never going to believe we're having a wild and passionate affair anyway,' said Caro, ruffled. 'He thinks I'm too boring for that.'

'Then why don't you show him just how wrong he is?' Philippe leant forward over the table and fixed Caro with his silver gaze. He really had extraordinary eyes, she found herself thinking irrelevantly. Wolf's eyes, their lightness accentuated by the darkness of his features and the fringe of black lashes. It was easier to think about that than about the way her heart was thudding in her throat at his nearness.

'How do you suggest I do that?' she said, struggling to hold on to her composure. 'We can hardly get down and dirty under the table!'

A faint contemptuous smile curled the corners of Philippe's mouth. 'Well, that would certainly make the point, but I was thinking of rather subtle ways of suggesting that we can't keep our hands off each other. For a start, you could keep your attention fixed on me, rather than on him! If we were really sleeping together, we'd be absorbed in each other.'

'It doesn't always have to be about you, you know,' grumbled Caro. 'Anyway, I *am* looking at you.' She fixed her eyes at him. 'There. Satisfied?'

'You could make it look as if you adore me and can't wait for me to drag you back to bed.'

'Oh, that's easy.' Caro summoned a suitably besotted expression and batted her lashes at him.

'What's the matter?' asked Philippe.

'Nothing's the matter! I'm looking adoring!'

'You look constipated,' he said frankly. 'Come on, you must be able to do better than that.'

'You're the expert on seduction,' said Caro, sulking. 'You do it.'

'OK.' Philippe reached across the table for her hand, turned it over and lifted it. 'Watch and learn,' he said, pressing a kiss into her palm.

Caro sucked in a breath as a current of warmth shot up her arm and washed through her. Her scalp was actually tingling with it. Bad sign. Willing the heat to fade, she struggled to keep her voice even.

'Oh, that old chestnut,' she said as lightly as she could. 'I would have done the hand-kissing thing, but I thought it would be too boring.'

'Kissing's never boring,' said Philippe. Now he was playing with her fingers, looking straight into her eyes, brushing his lips across her knuckles until she squirmed in her seat. 'Not the way we do it, anyway. Or that's what we want it to look like. We want everyone to think that we've just fallen out of bed, don't we? They ought to be looking at us and seeing that we can't keep our hands off each other. That we can't wait until we get home and I can undress you, very, very slowly, until you beg me to make love to you again.'

The sound of his voice and the tantalising caress of his fingers were doing alarming things to Caro. Heat was uncoiling in the pit of her belly and her mouth was dry. She had to get herself back under control.

'I never beg,' she said, but not nearly as steadily as she would have liked.

Philippe looked into her eyes and smiled. 'You do when you're with me.'

'I don't think so,' said Caro, but his smile only deepened.

She could see the candlelight flickering in the silver eyes, and her heart was thumping so loudly she was afraid the other diners would turn round and complain about the noise.

'Yes, you do, because I'm the only one who knows that behind closed doors you're a wild, passionate woman.' His voice was a tangible thing, velvet smoothing seductively over her skin. It would be so easy to succumb to it, to the warm, sure hands and the wickedly attractive smile, and Caro had to physically brace herself against it.

'Gosh, do women really fall for this stuff?' she asked.

'It's working, isn't it?'

For one horrible moment, Caro wondered if he could see her toes curling. 'Working?'

'You haven't been looking at what's-his-name at all.' It was true. She had completely forgotten about George for a while there. 'But he's been looking at you,' Philippe went on in the same disturbingly arousing voice, 'and he's very much afraid that you've found yourself a much, much better lover.'

Caro's eyes flickered to George, who was looking as if he'd been stuffed. Maybe there was something in this technique of Philippe's after all.

Philippe sat back smugly. 'And that's how it's done,' he said. 'Now you have a go.'

Her hand was throbbing where his lips had grazed her skin. Flustered by Philippe's abrupt transition from lover to teacher, Caro tucked the stray strands of hair behind her ears and assumed a nonchalance she wasn't feeling.

'Well, I *would*, but the food will be arriving any second and I don't want to spoil your appetite.'

'Coward,' he said softly. 'Besides, it's good practice for you. You're going to have to do better than screwing up your face if you're going to convince the Dowager Blanche that we're mad about each other.'

'Oh, all right.' Caro took a fortifying sip of her champagne and moistened her lips nervously while she thought, and saw Philippe's gaze fix on her mouth. She hadn't even started yet! Surely it couldn't be as easy as that?

Leaning forward, she rested her arms on the table, hugged them together and tried a seductive smile. She felt a fool, but Philippe's eyes dropped to her cleavage, and his eyes darkened unmistakably.

Encouraged, Caro felt around with her foot and managed to hook the toe of her shoe around his ankle. With a little manoeuvring, she could rub her foot tantalisingly up and down his calf. It felt awkward but it seemed to be working.

She waited for Philippe to burst out laughing, but he didn't. There was just the suspicion of a smile around his mouth as the light gaze returned to her face.

'How am I doing?' she asked.

'I think you may be a natural.'

Was he being sarcastic? Caro eyed him suspiciously but it was impossible to tell what he was really thinking.

It was a relief when their starters arrived and she could sit back. Funny, she had forgotten about how hungry she was while Philippe had been kissing her fingers. Now she picked up her fork to dig into her wild mushroom risotto and discovered that for possibly the only time in her life, her appetite had deserted her.

But Caro wasn't going to waste her one and only opportunity to eat at the Star and Garter. She made herself savour the food and refused to let herself think about Philippe sitting opposite her with his warm hands and his warm mouth.

'That was delicious,' she said, putting her fork down at last.

'Yes, it wasn't bad,' said Philippe indifferently. Michelin starred restaurants would be two a penny to him, of course. He held out his hand. 'Come on, back to looking besotted.'

'Must I?' sighed Caro, but she took his hand and, at the feel of his strong fingers curling around hers, a shiver of pleasure snaked through her.

Clearing her throat, she said, 'We ought to talk about practicalities.'

'Practicalities?'

To her consternation, Philippe turned her hand over so that the soft skin of her forearm was exposed. Now he was rubbing his thumb softly over her wrist, where her vein pulsed with awareness.

Caro swallowed hard and soldiered on. 'What's going to happen next?'

He would go back to Montluce in the next couple of days, Philippe told her. He would break the news about their supposed relationship to the Dowager Blanche and give Lotty a chance to make her own plans to leave. Then he would escort his father to Paris for his treatment.

'He won't want me, but he ought to have someone other than servants there for the operation,' he said. 'Once he's through that, I'll come and pick you up, and we'll go back to Montluce together. Will ten days or so be enough time for you to get ready?'

She nodded, desperately trying to ignore that stroking thumb, which was playing havoc with her breathing. 'I'm only temping,' she said unevenly. 'I just need to give a week's notice.'

'Once we're there, you won't have to do much,' Philippe said. 'Hang around with me. Convince my great-aunt that you adore me. Hold my hand like this. The usual stuff.'

'It doesn't sound very interesting,' said Caro austerely to cover the booming of her pulse.

'No, but it shouldn't be hard either.'

'Where—' She stopped, mortified by how high her voice sounded, and coughed. 'Where will I stay?' That was better, huskier, almost normal.

'With me,' said Philippe. 'We're not going to convince anyone that it's a serious relationship if we're not living together. I've got apartments in the palace in Montvivennes. Not where I'd choose to live, but it's comfortable enough.'

Apartments, plural? That sounded big. Caro was reassured. 'Plenty of space for both of us, then?'

'Oh, yes.' His eyes met hers, clearly knowing exactly the way her mind was going. 'Of course, we'll have to sleep together,' he said.

'That won't be necessary, surely?' Caro stiffened and tried to pull her hand away, but he held her tight. 'No one need know where I'm sleeping as long as I'm staying with you.'

'That's what you think.' Philippe's voice was crisp. 'There are servants in and out of the apartments all the time, and it would be a miracle if they didn't talk to each other. They'll wonder just what kind of relationship we have if we're not sleeping together, and word will get back. My great-aunt knows everything that goes on in the palace. She's got a spy network that would put the CIA to shame.'

'Couldn't we tell her you respect me too much to sleep with me before marriage?'

He offered her a sardonic smile in return. 'Yes, she'll believe that!'

Caro managed to tug her hand away at last. It was all very well for Philippe to sound coolly amused about the whole business, but he must have slept with millions of beautiful women. He was probably used to sleeping with strangers. The thought of sleeping with her clearly hadn't left *him* with an unnerving fluttering underneath his skin and in the pit of his stomach. *He* hadn't been misery-eating, so he didn't have to worry about what she would think when he took his clothes off.

Philippe naked…Caro's mind veered off track momentarily to imagine him pulling off his shirt with a grin. She could picture the lean, hard planes of his body with startling ease: the flex of his muscles under his skin, the broad chest, the flat stomach. The power and the grace and the sheer, sinful sexiness of him.

Her cheeks burned at the thought. She *really* didn't want her imagination to start running wild like that, especially not when taking off her own shirt would reveal all those extra pounds she had put on since George dumped her…and it wasn't as if she had been sylphlike to start with. No, there would be no undressing going on, under any circumstances.

'We can put a pillow down the middle, if you like,' said Philippe, apparently reading her mind without difficulty.

Without being aware of what she was doing, Caro cupped the wrist where he had stroked her with her free hand as if to calm the soft skin there, which was quivering still from his touch.

'You don't sound bothered one way or the other,' she said, unable to keep the snippiness from her voice.

He shrugged. 'I'm not. It's entirely up to you, Caro. I'm more than capable of keeping my hands to myself, so there's no need to panic.'

'I'm not panicking,' she said crossly. 'I'm just trying to think how it would work.'

She took her hand from her wrist and sat straighter. It was time to be sensible. 'If you say that we need to share a bed, then that's what we'll do. I'm not going to be silly about it. But I think sex would just confuse the issue,' she said, rather proud of her coolness this time. 'I think it would be easier if we agreed that we would be just friends while we're together.'

'Friends?' he repeated, expressionless.

'Yes, you know, when you have a good time but don't want to sleep together.'

'I've got friends,' he said. 'They're just not usually women.'

'There's nothing usual about our relationship, though, is

there, Philippe? You're a prince, I'm an ordinary girl with no interest in anything other than an ordinary life. You're wealthy by any standard, and I'm temping to pay my rent. You go out with beautiful, glamorous women, and I'm neither,' Caro said. 'We've got absolutely nothing in common apart from Lotty, but just for two months we're going to be together. I'm not interested in you, and I think it's pretty clear you're not going to be interested in me, so it makes sense that we should agree to be friends at least, don't you think?'

Why not? Philippe asked himself. Caro was right. It would be much easier this way. The last thing he wanted was to get involved with someone who would fall in love with him. That would complicate matters and it would all get very messy. There would be tears and scenes and demands for commitment and stormings off. Philippe had been there before, and he couldn't afford anything similar this time if he didn't want to be left at the mercy of the Dowager Blanche's matchmaking plans again.

So it was just as well Caro had made it clear that she wasn't interested in him. There was no need to feel nettled. It wasn't as if she was *his* type either. Caro was right: she wasn't beautiful, she wasn't stylish. She was untidy and distracting, that was all.

It was just that he couldn't shake the feel of her. When he'd put his arm around her to cross the restaurant, he'd rested his hand on the flare of her hip and felt the silky material of her dress shift over her skin with a shock of awareness. He'd held her wrist and felt the blood beating in her veins, and that, too, had been like a current thrilling through him. He looked away from her mouth.

'Fine by me,' he said, as carelessly as he could. 'Friends it is, and we'll get that pillow out as soon as we get there.'

Philippe was used to eating with women who automatically chose the least fattening meal on the menu and it was a revelation to watch Caro oohing and aahing over her choice. Philippe himself was largely indifferent to food—he reserved his passion for the wine list—but it was impossible not to enjoy eating with someone who took so much pleasure in it. Caro would close her eyes blissfully while she savoured every taste and texture. She loaded up forkfuls from her dish and insisted he try it, and reached over to help herself to a taste of his, until he suggested that they simply swap plates.

He was being sarcastic, but Caro was delighted at the suggestion and promptly handed over her plate. 'George always refused to share like this,' she confided. 'He said it was embarrassing to pass plates over the table and that everyone would look at us.'

'And this was a guy who accused *you* of not being any fun?'

'He probably swaps plates with Melanie,' she said with a sigh.

'You should have tried leaning over the table so that he could fall down your cleavage,' Philippe said. 'I'm sure he'd have swapped anything you wanted then.'

'Do you really think so?' The blue eyes rested wistfully on George and Philippe was conscious of a quite irrational stab of jealousy.

He was used to being the centre of attention. His dinner companions were invariably beautiful, just as Caro had said. They flirted and sparkled and charmed and laughed at all his jokes. It was a salutary experience to be with Caro, who was far more interested in her ex-fiancé than in him. She was more interested in the *food* than in him, come to that.

Philippe told himself that he was amused, but the truth was that he was just a little piqued by her indifference. Here was he, a prince famous for his charm and his wit and his sexual prowess, having to work to keep the attention of a woman who wasn't even really pretty, and who didn't feel the least need to keep him entertained. Not that he wanted to be entertained, of course, but still…

It was annoying to find that his leg was tingling where she had rubbed her shoe so tantalisingly, and that his eyes kept snagging on that mouth, or drifting to that luscious cleavage. Philippe suspected that Caro had no idea how she looked, with that provocative mouth and that wickedly lush body, so at odds with the combative glint in her blue eyes and the sharpness of her tongue.

I'm not interested in you, she had said.

Just as well.

For the first time in her life, Caro refused pudding. Finally, she'd made it to the Star and Garter, and she wasn't hungry! Life could be so unfair sometimes.

'Ready to go?' asked Philippe. 'Let's make sure we make an exit.' Very casually, he rested a hand at the nape of her neck as they passed George's table. It was a perfect proprietorial gesture, and it felt disturbingly intimate to Caro. The warmth from his fingers snaked down her spine, making her shiver.

'They'll be leaving any minute themselves,' Philippe murmured as he opened the door for her. 'Do you want to kiss me?'

'What?' Caro stopped dead and stared at him. 'No, of course not!'

'Sure? Because here's an opportunity to convince George that you're having a passionate affair, if you want to,' he said, all reasonableness. 'He *might* have been convinced by all the hand-holding, but it was all a bit tame, wasn't it? Whereas if he sees you enjoying a steamy kiss, there's not going to be much doubt in his mind that you're a passionate, exciting woman having a better time without him, is there?'

Caro hesitated. The idea of making George believe that she was in the throes of a wild affair was deeply appealing, she had to admit. For too long, she'd felt dull and repressed next to bubbly Melanie, and hated that deadly feeling that they both felt sorry for her.

But this was His Serene Highness Prince Philippe of Montluce... Did she really have the nerve to kiss him? On the other hand, they *had* agreed to be friends, hadn't they? 'Are you sure you wouldn't mind?' she asked doubtfully.

In reply, Philippe spread his arms. 'What are friends for? Besides, it'll be good practice for us. We're going to have to kiss in Montluce, so we might as well get used to it.'

True. Good point. Caro took a deep breath. 'Well...okay, then.'

'Come over here.' Philippe took her hand and led her over to the limousine, which waited in the glow of a single street light immediately opposite the door. 'There's no point if George can't see us, is there? They won't be able to miss us here.' He turned and leant back against the limousine. 'Off you go, then.'

'Where's Yan?'

'Don't worry about Yan. He's used to looking the other way.'

'Right.' Above them, the sky was a dark, dark blue, and the cool night air brimmed with the scents of a northern summer. A little current of excitement ran under Caro's skin. Moistening her lips, she stepped towards him, then hesitated.

'I feel silly.'

'That's because you're too far away. You'll find it easier if you get a bit closer.'

Caro took another step. It brought her up against him. She could smell his cologne—subtle, expensive—and, when she rested her palms against his chest, she felt the hard solidity of him through the fine material of his shirt.

The street lamp cast a surreal orange glow over everything, but at the same time Caro could see exactly what she was doing. It was like being on stage, and now she had to perform.

Gripped by shyness, she stared fixedly at Philippe's collar while her hands pressed against his chest and the warmth of his skin seemed to pulse through her, slow and steady like his heartbeat.

'I don't want to hurry you, but they'll be out soon,' said Philippe and his voice reverberated through her hands.

'Right,' she said again, and swallowed. Passionate, exciting…she could do it.

Forcing her eyes up from his collar, she let them drift up the strong column of his throat. She could see the faint prickle of stubble and, without giving herself time to think, she touched her lips to the pulse beating there.

Philippe inhaled slowly. His hands hung loosely by his sides, but she felt the tension in his body, and she smiled. Maybe he wasn't quite as cool as he made out.

Her heart was thudding painfully, *bang, bang, bang* against her ribs. She kissed the pulse again, then drifted soft kisses up to his jaw. It felt deliciously rough beneath her lips and she slid her hands to his shoulders.

'I think you'd better get on with it,' said Philippe, but a smile rippled through the words.

'Stop talking,' she mumbled, making her way along his chin. 'You're putting me off.'

'I'm just saying. George will be out any second.'

Caro pulled away, exasperated. 'I can't do it if you're going to do a running commentary!'

'Then make me stop talking,' he challenged her.

'Fine.' Defiantly, she stepped back up to him and put her hands on his shoulders once more. Then she leant into him, angling her face up and pressing her mouth against his. His lips were warm and firm and relaxed and curved into the faintest of smiles.

Was he laughing at her? Caro kissed him again, nibbling little kisses at the edge of his mouth where his smile dented, teasing his lips open so that their tongues could twine together, and it felt so warm, so right, that she forgot everything else. She forgot George and Melanie. She forgot the plan. She forgot about just being friends. There was only the taste of him and the feel of him and the astonishing sweetness spilling through her.

Then Philippe's arms closed round her at last and he pulled her hard against him, and the sweetness was swept away by a surge of heat. It was wild and dark and fierce, a current that swirled around them, sucking them down, pulling them off their feet. Caro was lost, tumbling in the frantic wash of desire. She linked her arms around his neck to anchor herself, murmuring low in her throat, something inarticulate that might have been protest, or might have been longing.

Somehow Philippe had found the clip in her hair and pulled it free. It fell, unnoticed, to the ground while he slid his fingers through the silky mass, twisting, twining, holding her head still so that he could kiss her back, and he was good, oh, he was good…Caro thrilled at the sureness of his lips, the hard insistence of his hands that slid down her spine to cup her bottom and lift her against him.

She could feel his arousal, and she pulled her mouth from his so that she could gasp for breath.

'Philippe…'

She wasn't even sure what she meant to say, but Philippe, who was kissing her throat and making her shiver with delight at the heat and the hunger of it, stilled as if she had whacked him across the head.

Caro felt him draw a ragged breath, then another. 'Good God,' he said, sounding shaken, and let her go. 'Maybe that's enough practice for now.'

Practice? Desperately, Caro tried to bring her scattered senses back under control. She needed a decompression chamber, somewhere to learn to breathe again, a staging post between heady pleasure and the slap of reality where there was no touch, no taste, no feel, no giddy swing of the senses but only the chill of standing alone on a summer's night remembering that none of it had been real.

CHAPTER FOUR

MONTLUCE was such a tiny country that it didn't even have its own airport, so they were to fly to France and drive the rest of the way. In Caro's experience, flying meant a lot of queuing, a lot of delays, a lot of shuffling onto a crowded plane and shifting impatiently for the inevitable passenger who blocked the aisle for long minutes while he fussed about stashing away his duty-free in the overhead lockers.

Flying with Philippe was very different. The limousine he'd sent to pick her up in Ellerby that morning bypassed the terminal and deposited her right by the plane on the tarmac. Her bags were whisked away while Caro climbed out and stood looking dubiously up at the private jet. It looked very small. The wind was whipping tendrils of hair around her face and plastering them against her lips as fast as she could pull them free.

She was very nervous.

And cross with herself for feeling that way. Everything was going ahead exactly as they'd planned. Lotty was ecstatically grateful and would be gone before Caro and Philippe arrived. Once in Montluce, there would just be the two of them.

Which would be *fine*, Caro told herself. They had agreed to be friends, hadn't they? If it hadn't been for that stupid kiss…

But she wasn't supposed to be thinking about that. It had

been a mistake, they'd agreed afterwards. Both of them had been carried away by the pretence, but pretence was all it had been. It wasn't as if it had been a real kiss.

The trouble was that it had *felt* real. The firm curve of his mouth, his breath against her skin, the insistence of the sure hands cupping her buttocks and pulling her into him...oh, yes, it had felt real, all right. She could still feel the glittery rush, the heat. Philippe had been so hard, so surprisingly solid, so *male*. Every time Caro thought about him, her muscles would clench and a disturbing sensation, half shiver, half shudder, would snake its way down her spine.

Not that she would make the mistake of believing it had meant anything to Philippe. Just because she could admit he was attractive didn't mean that she was going to lose her mind. Caro might be many things, but she wasn't a fool.

After announcing their relationship to a relieved Lotty and a furious Dowager Blanche, Philippe had escorted his equally disappointed father to Paris to start his treatment, but for the last three or four days he'd been in London. Caro knew this because she'd seen his picture in *Glitz*. He'd been snapped coming out of a nightclub with Francesca Allen. Usually referred to as 'Britain's favourite actress', Francesca was famously beautiful, famously intelligent, famously nice— and famously married. The tabloids were having a field day speculating about what they were doing together.

It was a stupid thing to have done, given everything Philippe had had to say about convincing the Dowager Blanche that he was serious about *her*, Caro thought, and told herself that was the only reason she was feeling monumentally miffed. She wasn't silly enough to be jealous. *I'm more than capable of keeping my hands to myself*, Philippe had said, and Caro had no problem believing him, kiss or no kiss. A man like Philippe, used to hanging around with beautiful women the likes of Francesca Allen, was hardly likely to be tempted by an ordinary, overweight, eccentrically dressed Caroline Cartwright, was he?

No, being friends was the only way to get through the next few weeks. As a friend, she wouldn't have to worry about what she looked like, and there would be no need to feel twitchy about other, far more beautiful, women prowling around him. She could relax and enjoy herself with a friend.

Caro had barely reminded herself of that when Philippe appeared, ducking out of the cabin, long and lean and tautly muscled in a pale yellow polo shirt and chinos, and the breath whooshed out of her. He looked the same, and yet different, more *immediate* somehow: the cool mouth, the winged brows, the crisp line of his jaw, the startling contrast between the icy eyes and the darkness of his hair.

It must be something to do with the brightness of the light, the freshness of the breeze. Why else would the sight of him sharpen her senses and make her feel as if every cell in her body was alert and tingling?

At the top of the steps, Philippe looked down at Caro and was startled by how pleased he was to see her.

Of course, it would have been horribly awkward if she'd changed her mind, Philippe told himself. His announcement that he was bringing a girlfriend no one had ever heard of back to Montluce hadn't gone down well, to say the least, and he'd been subjected to endless harangues on the subject from his great-aunt, while his father had retreated into bitter disappointment as usual. Only Lotty, hugging him with a speaking look of gratitude, had stopped him from telling them what they could all do with their duty and responsibility and booking himself on the first plane back to Buenos Aires.

Philippe had been glad to escape to London and enjoy his last few days of freedom for a while. He'd met up with friends, played polo at the Guards Club, been to parties and dinners and renewed his acquaintance with the beautiful Francesca

Allen. He wasn't looking forward to the next six months, and couldn't decide whether this mad pretence with Caro Cartwright was going to make things better or worse. She was so different from the other women he knew. Not beautiful, not glamorous. Just ordinary. And yet Philippe had been surprised at how vividly he remembered her.

How vividly he remembered that kiss.

He'd been prepared for awkwardness, not for sweetness. Not for softness a man could lose himself in if he wasn't careful.

The memory made Philippe uncomfortable. He didn't do losing himself. But he'd been taken unawares by the way the dress slipped over her skin. The heat shooting through him had sucked the air from his brain, and the message to step back and keep his cool hadn't reached his hands.

Or his mouth.

Or the rest of him.

Philippe didn't understand it. Caro Cartwright ought to be the last woman to have that kind of effect on him. She wasn't even pretty, and as for her clothes…! Today she wore jeans and boots, with a plain white T-shirt, which wouldn't have looked too bad if she hadn't spoiled it by wearing an oversize man's dinner jacket over the top, its sleeves rolled up to show a brilliant scarlet lining. At least she was tall enough to carry it off with a certain panache, he allowed grudgingly.

No, Caro wasn't his type at all.

And yet there she stood, blue eyes wary and all that hair blowing around her face, and his heart unmistakably lifted.

Odd.

'There you are,' he said, pushing the discomfited feeling aside. It was too late to change his mind now. He went down the steps to greet her. 'I was beginning to wonder if you'd changed your mind.'

'I did think about it,' Caro confessed. 'But then I heard

from mutual friends that George is worried I might be going off the rails. He's obviously found out who you were, and he thinks you've got a bad reputation,' she said cheerfully. 'Now he's afraid that I'm going to do something stupid and get hurt—and, as we all know, he's the only one allowed to hurt me! So I thought I'd come after all, and send lots of messages home to make sure he knows what a glamorous time I'm having while Melanie is going to the supermarket and making George his tea the way he likes it. Then we'll see who's having the most fun, fun, fun!'

'Excellent,' said Philippe. 'In that case, you'd better come aboard.'

Caro was deeply impressed by the inside of the plane, which was fitted out with six plush leather seats, wall-to-wall carpeting and a lot of polished wood. Yan was already there, sitting in the cockpit.

'Take a seat,' Philippe said. 'Now you're here, we're ready to go.'

Caro looked around. 'Where's the pilot?'

'You're looking at him.'

'You're not a pilot!'

'I'm not? Then we're going to be in trouble because there's no one else to fly the plane.'

'I'm serious,' said Caro uneasily as she sat down in the seat nearest the front. 'Are you sure you know how to fly?'

Philippe settled himself in the cockpit and began flicking switches. 'Sure. I did a five-minute course a few years ago.'

'Really?'

'No, of course not really!' he said, exasperated. 'You don't think they let you in the air unless you're properly qualified, do you?'

'They might if you can stick Prince in front of your name,' said Caro with a dark look, although she was reassured to see Yan beside him. Surely he wouldn't let Philippe fly unless he knew what he was doing? 'The rules don't usually apply to people like you.'

'Well, in this case they do,' said Philippe. 'I've got a licence, I assure you. What do you think I've been doing for the past few years?'

'I don't know. Playing polo?'

'Pah! Who wants to get on a horse when you can fly a plane?'

'What, you mean you just get in your plane and fly around in the sky?' It seemed a bit pointless to Caro.

'No, I fly to places,' he said, his hands busy checking dials and switches. Caro just hoped he knew what he was doing.

'What places?' she asked suspiciously.

'I go wherever a plane is needed. I've got a friend who organises logistics for a number of aid organisations. They might need a development worker transported in a remote village, or tents dropped after an earthquake…if you haven't got the time or the money to get through the bureaucratic red tape, I'm your man.'

Philippe glanced over his shoulder at Caro. 'It gives me something to do when I'm bored,' he said, as if he feared he might have given too much of himself away. 'And it's more fun than polo! Now, fasten your seat belt while we finish the pre-flight check here.'

He turned back to the controls. 'Er, what's this red button again?' he pretended to ask Yan. 'Oh, right, the eject seat. Oops, better avoid that one! So the start button must be…oh, yes, I remember now. All right in the back there?' he called over his shoulder to Caro.

'Ha, ha, ha,' she said in a monotone. 'That's a fake laugh, by the way!'

'Relax,' he said. 'I hardly ever crash. Besides, I thought you'd decided to have fun, fun, fun, and what could be more fun than flying around in a private jet?'

'It won't be much fun when the plane crashes,' she grumbled.

The plane didn't crash, of course, but it felt as if something even more disastrous was happening inside her as she watched Philippe push the throttle remorselessly forwards. His long hands were absolutely steady as they shot along the runway, and Caro's stomach dropped away as the plane lifted into the air.

She was more impressed than she wanted to admit. Why had she assumed that he had been living an idle trust fund existence? She should have realised that a man like Philippe would be bored with nothing to do but party all day. There was that reckless edge to him that she had noticed even as a boy. It was all too easy to imagine him flying planes into war zones, dodging bullets or volcanic ash or pot-holed runways. He would thrive on the danger.

Philippe had been very quick to dismiss what he did, Caro had noticed. *Something to do when I'm bored*, he had said. There must be plenty of other jaded rich people out there, but how many of them would risk their lives for others the way he did? Philippe could get his thrills racing cars or helicopter skiing or doing any of the other extreme sports that catered to the very rich and very bored, but instead he flew his plane where it was needed. No doubt he did enjoy it, but Caro thought it was more than possible that he would go anyway.

She liked that about him, and she liked the fact that he clearly didn't publicise what he was doing. He wasn't like so many other celebrities, using charity work to raise their own profiles. Caro wondered if even Lotty knew.

From where she sat, she could see the hard edge of Philippe's jaw, the flash of his smile as he turned to speak to Yan beside him. Caro could see one powerfully muscled arm. Her eyes drifted from the dark, flat hairs on his forearm to the broad, strong wrist, and on to the firm fingers holding the joystick, and a disquieting ache stirred low in her belly.

She made herself look away, out of the window. The seat was pressing into the small of her back as they climbed up through great blowsy drifts of clouds, up into the blue. There was no going back to real life now. Instead, she would spend the next two months as Philippe's girlfriend. Caro's eyes slid back to his profile, etched now against the bright sky. She could see the creases at the edge of his eye, the corner of his mouth, and remembering how warm and sure it had felt against her own made her stomach tilt anew.

Two months beside him. Two months trying not to notice the cool set of his mouth or remember the feel of his hands.

The squirmy feeling in Caro's belly intensified. Nerves, she decided at first, but when she looked out at the clouds and felt the plane soaring upwards and thought about the weeks ahead she finally recognised the feeling for what it was.

Excitement.

'Oh, what a beautiful car!' Caro gasped when she saw the Aston Martin waiting for them at the quiet airfield where they landed. Philippe watched her practically fall down the steps in her eagerness to get at it.

Unless it was her eagerness to get out of the plane, of course.

'Oh, you beauty!' she said, running a hand lovingly over the bonnet. 'A DB9! I've never seen one before.' She looked up at him, her eyes shining. 'Is it yours?'

'It is.' She was so vivid standing there in the sunlight, her face alight with enthusiasm, that Philippe's breath hitched in a new and disturbing way, and for a moment he couldn't remember how to be.

'This isn't like you.' Ah, yes, that was better. Cool, indifferent. That was him. 'You know the car's not second-hand, don't you? And you can't eat it? I wouldn't have thought it was your kind of thing at all.'

'I make an exception for cars.' Caro let her hand smooth over the bodywork in a way that made Philippe's throat dry ridiculously. He fought for a casual expression, but all he could think, bizarrely, was: *lucky car.*

'Can I drive?' she asked, with a speculative look from under her lashes, trying it on.

'Absolutely not,' he said firmly.

'Oh, please! I'll behave very, very nicely.'

'No.'

'You're supposed to be in love with me,' she pointed out as she straightened.

'I'd have to be besotted before I let you drive my car,' he said, and opened the passenger door for her. 'Most girls would be happy to be driven.'

'I'm not most girls,' said Caro, but she got in anyway and he closed the door after her with a satisfying clunk.

'You can say that again,' said Philippe, walking round to get in behind the wheel. Now she was stroking the seat and the wooden trim, leaning forward to gaze at the dashboard, wriggling back into her seat with a sigh of pleasure. It was practically pornographic! Not enough oxygen was getting to his brain and he had to take a breath, horrified to find that the hands he laid on the steering wheel weren't entirely steady.

The clear glass starter button glowed invitingly red, reminding him that he was in control. Philippe pressed it and the engine purred into life.

'What about Yan and the luggage?' Caro dragged her attention back from the car for a moment.

'He'll follow in the other car,' said Philippe, nodding back to a black SUV with tinted windows.

'Isn't he supposed to be protecting you?'

'He'll be right behind.' Philippe put the car into gear. 'But for now it's just you and me.'

'Oh,' was all Caro said, but a little thrill shivered through her all the same.

Just you and me.

It wouldn't be just the two of them, of course. Lotty had told her about the palace servants, and there would always be Yan or a member of the public wanting their hand shaken. Just as well, Caro told herself firmly. It would be much easier to be friends when there were other people around.

'Where did you learn about cars?' Philippe asked as they turned onto the main road.

'From my father.' The road was clear ahead, and Philippe put his foot down. The car responded instantly, surging forward. Caro felt the pressure in the small of her back and settled into it with a shiver of pleasure. 'He loved cars. He always had some banger up on the blocks and he'd spend hours tinkering with it. When I was little I'd squat beside him and be allowed to hand him a spanner or an oily rag. Even now the smell of oil makes me think of Dad.'

Caro smiled unevenly, remembering. 'Driving an Aston Martin was his dream. He'd be so thrilled if he could see me now!' She stroked the leather on either side of her thighs. 'And envious!'

Distracted by the stroking, Philippe forced his attention back to the road. 'It sounds like you had a good relationship with your father.'

'I adored him.' She touched the lapels of the jacket she wore. 'This is Dad's dinner jacket. He wore it for a school dance once, and no one recognised him. It was as if none of them had ever looked at him when he was wearing his handyman overalls, but put on a smart jacket and suddenly he was a real person, someone they could talk to because he was dressed like them.'

Caro fingered the sleeve where she'd rolled it up to show the scarlet lining. 'I remember Dad saying that some people are like this jacket, conventional on the outside, but with a bright, beautiful lining like this. He said we shouldn't judge what's on the outside, it's what's inside that really matters. I think of him every time I put this jacket on,' she said.

'My father thinks the exact opposite,' said Philippe. 'For him, it's *all* about appearances. No wonder I'm such a disappointment to him.' He was careful to keep his tone light, but Caro looked at him, a crease between her brows.

'He can't be that disappointed if he trusts you to stand in for him while he's sick.'

'Only because it wouldn't look right if he didn't make his only surviving son regent in his absence, would it? What would people *think*?'

In spite of himself, Philippe could hear the bitterness threading his voice, and he summoned a smile instead. 'Besides, it's not a question of trust. It's not as if they're going to let me loose on government. My father thinks it'll be good for me to experience meetings and red boxes and the whole dreary business of governing, but all that's just for show too. There's a council of ministers, but the Dowager Blanche will be keeping a firm hold of the reins. I'm trusted to shake hands and host a few banquets, but that's about it.'

'You could take more responsibility if you wanted, couldn't you?'

'They won't let me.' Caro could hear the frustration in his voice, and she felt for him. It couldn't be easy knowing that any attempt to assert himself would be met by his father's collapse. 'And I daren't risk insisting any more,' Philippe said. 'Not when he's so sick, anyway. My father and I may not get on, but I don't want him to die.'

'Why doesn't he trust you?' Caro asked, swivelling in her seat so that she could look at him. 'I know you were wild when you were younger, but that was years ago.'

'It's hard to change the way your family looks at you.'

Philippe glanced in the mirror and pulled out to overtake a lumbering truck in a flash. 'Etienne was always the dutiful, responsible son, and I was difficult. That's just the way it was.

'Etienne was a golden boy—clever, hard-working, responsible, handsome, charming, kind. I could never live up to him, so I never tried. I was only ever "the spare" in my father's eyes, anyway,' he said. 'I didn't even have the good sense to look like him, the way Etienne did. Instead, I take after my mother. Every time my father looks at me, he's reminded of the way she humiliated him. I sometimes wonder if he suspects I'm not even his son.'

Philippe hoped that he sounded detached and ironic, but suspected it didn't fool Caro, who was watching him with those warm blue eyes. He could feel her gaze on his profile as surely as if she had reached out to lay her palm against his cheek.

'I never heard anything about your mother,' she said. 'What did she do?'

'Oh, the usual. She was far too young and frivolous to have been married to my father. It's a miracle their marriage lasted as long as it did. She ran away from him eventually and went to live with an Italian racing driver.'

He thought he had the tone better there. Careless. Cynical. Just a touch of amusement.

'Do you remember her?'

'Not much,' he said. 'Her perfume when she came to kiss me goodnight. Her laughter. I was only four, and left with a nanny a lot of the time anyway, so I don't suppose it made much difference to me really when she left. It was worse for Etienne. He was eleven, so he must have had more memories of her.'

Philippe paused. 'He would have been devastated, but he

used to come and play with me for hours so that I wouldn't miss her. That was the kind of boy he was.'

'I didn't realise you were so close to him.'

Caro's throat was aching for the little boy Philippe had been. Her father had been right. You could never tell what someone was like from the face they put on to the world. All she'd ever seen of Philippe had been the jacket of cool arrogance. It had never occurred to her to wonder whether he used it to deflect, to stop anyone realising that he had once been a small boy, abandoned by his mother and rejected by his father.

'He was a great brother,' said Philippe. 'A great person. You can't blame my father for being bitter that Etienne was the one who died, and that he was left with me. You can't blame him for wishing that I'd been the one who died.'

'That's…that's a terrible thing to say,' said Caro, shocked.

'It's true.' He glanced at her and then away. 'It was my fault Etienne died.'

'No.' Caro put out an instinctive hand. 'No, it was an accident. Lotty told me.'

'Oh, yes, it was an accident, but if it hadn't been for me, he'd never have been on the lake that day.' The bleak set to Philippe's mouth tore at her heart. 'Lotty's father was Crown Prince, and his brother still alive, with his two sons,' he went on after a moment. 'There was no reason to believe we'd ever inherit. My father had a vineyard, and Etienne was going up to look at the accounts or something equally tedious. He envied me, he said. To him it seemed that I was the one always having a good time. He said he wished he could do the same, but he was afraid that he didn't have the courage.'

He overtook a car, and then another and another, the sleek power of the Aston Martin controlled utterly in his strong hands.

'"Come water skiing with me", I said,' he remembered

bitterly. '"For once in your life, do what *you* want to do instead of what our father wants you to do." So he did, and he died.'

'It wasn't your fault,' said Caro.

'My father thinks it was.'

'It wasn't.' Without thinking, she put her hand on his shoulder. Through the yellow polo shirt, she could feel his muscles corded with tension. 'It was Etienne's choice to go. You didn't make him fall, and you didn't kill him. It was an accident.'

'That was what Lotty said. She was the only one who stood by me then,' said Philippe. 'If it had been up to my father, I wouldn't even have been allowed to go to the funeral. "If it wasn't for you, Etienne would still be alive," he said. The Dowager Blanche persuaded him to let me go in the end, for *appearance's sake*.' His voice was laced with pain.

'As soon as it was over, I left for South America. I didn't care where I went, as long as it was a long way from Montluce, and my father felt exactly the same. If it hadn't been for inheriting the throne, he'd have been happy never to see me again, I think, but when he became Crown Prince, he didn't have much choice but to be in touch. He'll never be able to forgive me, though, for the fact that Etienne didn't have time to get married and secure the succession.

'There's a certain irony in that,' Philippe said with a sidelong glance at Caro. 'Etienne was gay. He was very, very discreet, and my father never found out.'

'You didn't tell him?'

'How could I? It would have destroyed him all over again. All he's got left is his image of Etienne as his perfect son. I'm not going to spoil that for him. It wouldn't bring Etienne back and, anyway, he *was* perfect and, clearly, I'm not.'

'But why don't you tell him that you've changed?'

'Who says that I have?'

'The old Philippe wouldn't have flown in emergency supplies,' said Caro, and he lifted a shoulder.

'It would take more than a few flights to change my father's view of me,' he said. 'My father isn't a bad man, and if it's easier for him to keep thinking of me as difficult, why should I insist that he changes his mind? He's had enough grief without me demanding his attention and approval. I'm not a child,' said Philippe.

'I think it's unfair,' said Caro stoutly. 'I think if they're going to make you regent, they should give you the responsibility to act too.'

'Lots of people live with unfairness, Caro. I've seen people struggling to get by without food or shelter or a stable government. They haven't got schools or hospitals. There's no running water. *That's* unfair,' he said. 'Compared to that, I think I can bear a few months of not being allowed to make decisions. I'll use the time to familiarise myself with how the government works and then, when I'm in a position to make a difference, I will. Until then, I can live with a few pointless rituals.'

Caro was still looking dubious. 'It's not going to be much fun for you, is it?'

'No,' said Philippe, 'but we're not there yet.' Leaning across, he turned up the volume on the sound system and slanted a smile at her. 'We've got about an hour until we hit the border. Let's make the most of being able to behave badly while we can, shall we?'

Caro never forgot that drive. The poplars on either side of the road barred the way with shadows, so that the sunlight flickered exhilaratingly as the car shot beneath them with a throaty roar, effortlessly gobbling up the miles and sliding around the bends as if it were part of the road.

The sky was a hot, high blue. Cocooned in comfort, enveloped in the smell of new leather and luxury, she leant back in her seat and smiled. The windscreen protected her from the worst of the wind, but a heady breeze stirred her hair and she could feel the sun striping her face while the insistent beat of the music pounded through her and made her feel wild and excited and *alive*.

She was preternaturally aware of Philippe driving, of the flex of his thigh when he pressed the clutch, the line of his jaw, the alertness of his eyes checking between the road and the mirror. He changed gear with an assurance that was almost erotic, and she had to force herself to look away.

Caro could have driven on for ever that morning, her face flushed with wind and sun and Philippe beside her, with that long, lean, powerful body, his smile flashing, his hands rock-steady on the wheel, but all too soon he was slowing and reaching out to turn the music off.

'Time to behave, I'm afraid,' he said. 'This is it.'

Tucked away in the mountains, Montluce was one of Europe's forgotten back waters, cut off from the great traffic routes where borders flashed past in the blink of an eye. Not only was there a real border with a barrier across the road, but there were two guards in braided uniforms. Caro began to dig around in her bag for her passport as Philippe slowed down.

'You won't need that,' said Philippe. 'This is my border, remember?'

The guards came sharply to attention when they recognised Philippe, who stopped long enough to exchange a few words in French with them. Caro watched the men relax. There was some laughter before they saluted smartly and, at a word from the officer, the junior guard leapt to open the barrier.

Philippe acknowledged his salute as he drove through. 'What?' he said, feeling Caro staring at him.

'That's the first time I've realised that you're royal,' she said. 'I mean, I knew you were, of course, but I hadn't *seen* it. Those men were *saluting* you!'

'You'd better get used to it,' Philippe said. 'Montluce is big on formality. A lot of bowing and curtseying and saluting goes on.'

'But you knew what to do.' Caro didn't know how to explain what a revelation it had been to see the assurance with which Philippe had received the salutes, how clearly he had been able to put the guards at their ease without losing his authority. Even casually dressed, there was no mistaking the prince. That was when it had struck her.

He was a prince.

CHAPTER FIVE

PHILIPPE might say Montluce didn't mean much to him, but a subtle change came over him as they drove up into the hills. Caro puzzled over what it was, until she realised that he looked at home. Perhaps it had been hearing him speak French. His English was so flawless that it was easy to forget that he wasn't British, but here he looked more Gallic than usual, his gestures more Continental.

It was a beautiful country, with wooded hills soaring into mountains whose bare tops glared in the sun. The smell of pines filled the drowsy air as they drove through picturesque villages, past rushing rivers and up winding roads dappled with the light through the trees. Caro felt as if she were driving into a magical kingdom, and she was sure of it when they came over the range and saw the valley spread out below them. A large lake gleamed silver between the mountains and the city of Montvivennes on the other. Caro could see the palace, a fairy tale confection with turrets and terraces made of pale elegant stone, and she couldn't prevent a gasp.

From a distance, it could have been made of spun sugar, mirrored serenely in the lake. She wouldn't have been at all surprised to see princesses leaning out of the towers, goblins guarding the gate and princes hacking their way through rose thickets. There would be wicked stepmothers and fairy godmothers, pumpkins that turned into coaches, wolves that climbed into bed and licked their lips when Little Red Riding Hood knocked at the door.

'Please tell me there's a tame dragon,' she said.

'Well, there's my great-aunt,' Philippe said, 'but I wouldn't call her tame.'

Montvivennes was an attractive city with the same timeless air as the palace. It seemed almost drowsy in the sunshine, the only jarring note being a group of protestors with placards clustered beside the main road that led up to the palace.

Caro tried to read the placards as they passed. 'What are they protesting about?'

'There's a proposal to put a gas line through Montluce,' said Philippe. 'They're worried about the environmental impact.'

A few moments later, they drove through the palace gates to more saluting and presenting of arms and came to a halt with a satisfying crunch of gravel in a huge courtyard.

'Wow,' said Caro.

Close to, the palace was less whimsical but much more impressive. The imposing front opened onto a square with plane trees. Behind, long windows opened onto terraces and formal gardens leading down to the lake, beyond which the hills piled up in the distance to the mountains.

Philippe switched off the engine and there was a moment of utter stillness. Caro saw two ornately dressed footmen standing rigidly at the top of the steps. It all felt unreal. Any minute now she was going to wake up. She wasn't really here with a prince, about to walk into his palace.

And then the footmen were coming down the steps, opening the car doors, and somehow Caro found herself standing on the gravel looking up at the elaborate doorway.

'Ready?' Philippe muttered out of the corner of his mouth as he came round to take her arm.

'Oh, my God.' Caro was frozen by a sudden surge of panic. 'Do you think we can really do this?'

Philippe put a smile on his face and urged her towards the steps. 'We're about to find out,' he said.

It wasn't your usual homecoming, that was for sure. No family members hurried out to greet them with a hug. Instead, they passed through serried ranks of servants, all dressed in knee breeches and coats with vast quantities of gold braid. Caro was all for vintage clothes, but that was ridiculous.

Philippe greeted all of them easily, not at all daunted by the formality. Caro's French wasn't up to much, but she caught her name and it was obvious that he was introducing her, so she smiled brightly and tried to look as if she might conceivably be the kind of girl Philippe would fall madly in love with.

She trotted along behind Philippe as they were led ceremonially to his apartments, trying hard not to be intimidated by the palace. It was decorated with the extravagant splendour which, like the footmen's livery, had been all the rage in the eighteenth century. There were sweeping staircases, vast glittering chandeliers, marble floors, massive oil paintings and lot of gilded and uncomfortable-looking Baroque furniture.

There were an awful lot of long corridors, too. 'It's like being in an airport,' Caro whispered to Philippe, 'and having to walk miles to the gate. You should think about having one of those moving walkways put in.'

Of course, airports didn't have footmen placed outside every room, presumably so that no member of the royal family would have to go to the effort of opening a door for themselves. As Philippe appeared, they would get to their feet and stand to attention, only to sink back onto their chairs when he had passed with a nod of acknowledgement. It was like a very slow Mexican wave.

Philippe's apartments were on the second floor of one of the palace wings. They were airy, gracious rooms, most with views out over the lake to the mountains beyond, but impersonally decorated.

'Home, sweet temporary home,' said Philippe, looking around him without enthusiasm.

'It's not exactly cosy, is it?' Caro was wandering around the room, touching things and feeling ridiculously self-conscious. The rooms were huge, but knowing that there were all those servants outside the door made it feel as if she and Philippe had been shut away together.

Just you and me.

They certainly weren't going to be cramped. There was a large sitting room, a dining room with a beautifully equipped but untouched kitchen behind a breakfast bar, a study and three bedrooms, each with a luxurious en suite bathroom.

'And this is our love nest,' said Philippe and opened the last door with a mock flourish.

'Oh.' Caro made an effort of unconcern but all she could see was the huge bed. The bed where she was going to sleep with Philippe tonight. The fluttering started again in the pit of her stomach.

'Plenty of pillows, as you can see.' Philippe's voice was Martini dry. 'And the bed is wide enough to put one down the middle if you're feeling twitchy.'

She was, but no power on earth would have made her admit it.

I'm more than capable of keeping my hands to myself.

'You said yourself that won't be necessary,' she managed. 'I'm sure you have more experience than I do of these situations.'

'I don't know about that. The pillow question hasn't come up very often before, I must admit.'

No, because the women Philippe took to bed would be sexy, sophisticated and size six at the most. They wouldn't have to worry about holding in their tummies. Their legs would always be waxed, their nail polish unchipped, their skin perfect. Caro was prepared to bet they never, ever dribbled into their pillows or woke up with mascara rings under their eyes.

'But then, you don't usually sleep with someone like me, do you?'

'No,' he said slowly. 'That's true.'

It was odd seeing her here, in her father's old jacket. She was completely out of place in all the baroque splendour, but her eyes were a deep blue and the sun through the window cast a halo of gold around the cloud of hair that tumbled to her shoulders. The formal apartments were warmer and more welcoming with Caro in them.

Philippe remembered quite clearly dismissing the idea that he might want to sleep with Caro. But that was before he'd kissed her. It didn't seem nearly so unlikely now.

She had wandered over to the window and stood there looking out, hugging the jacket around her so that he could see the flare of her hips. Her legs were strong and straight in the jeans. There was nothing special about her, not really. Other girls had blue eyes and creamy skin and hair that felt like silk when he slid his fingers through it. Caro was lusher than most, warmer than most, more vibrant than most, but she was still just an ordinary girl, Philippe reminded himself. Not the sort of girl he desired at all.

'I won't lay a finger on you unless you ask me to,' he said. 'So you can relax.'

'Oh, sure,' said Caro, turning from the window. 'Great idea. Relax. After all, I'm in a strange country, living in a palace and I'll be going to bed with a prince tonight. What on earth have I got to be nervous about?'

Philippe rolled his eyes at her sarcasm. 'Nothing,' he said. 'We're friends, remember?'

He could see her remembering that had been her idea. 'Yes,' she conceded reluctantly at last.

'And friends trust each other, don't they?'

'Ye...es.'

'So you're going to have to trust me when I say you've got nothing to worry about.'

Caro stood there, chewing her lip. 'You're right,' she said after a moment. 'I'm sorry.'

'Well, now we've got that sorted, we can get on,' said Philippe briskly. 'We've been summoned to an audience with the Dowager Blanche at four o'clock. Sadly, saying we're busy is not an option. At some time I need to see my father's equerry, too, but what would you like to do until then?'

Caro looked hopeful. 'Have lunch?' she said.

To: charlotte@palaisdemontvivennes.net
From: caro.cartwright@u2.com
Subject: I'm here...where are you?

Dear Lotty

I was going to ask where you are, but then it might be better if you didn't tell me, as I might not be able to withstand your grandmother's interrogation. She's pretty scary, isn't she?

Philippe took me to meet her today—oh, no, that's right, I didn't meet her, I was presented. And I had to learn how to curtsey! Philippe gave me a whole lesson on etiquette before we went. I suppose you take it all for granted, but I was completely bamboozled by everything I had to remember. I was really nervous, and I think Philippe was too. He had that aloof look on his face, the one that doesn't give anything away, but I noticed that on the way there (a five mile trek along the palace corridors, or that's what it felt like) he kept shooting his cuffs and running his finger around his collar as if it was too tight. He'd changed into a suit for the Dowager Blanche, and I must say he looked pretty good, although I didn't give him the satisfaction of saying that, of course. Philippe knows perfectly well how attractive he is, without me puffing him up any more.

Caro lifted her fingers from the keyboard and flexed them as she reread what she had written. Was there too much about Philippe in there? She didn't want Lotty getting the wrong idea. But how could she not mention him? She'd better make it clear that they had a strictly platonic relationship.

We've decided to be friends, which is great because it means we don't have to be polite to each other. He's certainly not polite about me. I put on my best dress in honour of the occasion (you know, the apple-green tea dress I bought last year) and he was beastly about it. I won't repeat what he said, but it was very rude. And I won't repeat what I said to him in return, because that was even ruder!

There, that sounded suitably casual and friendly, didn't it? Caro started typing again.

Anyway, back to the Dowager. She doesn't exactly operate an open door policy, does she? When we finally made it to her apartments, we had to go through endless antechambers, each one bigger than the last, and naturally we never had to do anything demeaning like opening a door ourselves. Instead, there was a whole army of footmen whose sole job seems to be to fling open doors. Weird. (Or maybe it seems perfectly natural to you???)

We eventually found ourselves facing your grand-mother across acres of polished parquet. Philippe didn't tell me about that, and I'd worn my pink shoes, the ones with the kitten heels. BIG mistake! The floor was so slippy the best I could manage was a teeter and we'd just about made it when my foot skidded out beneath me. I would have fallen splat on my face if Philippe hadn't grabbed my arm. He's pretty quick when he wants to be, isn't he? I was mortified, but then I looked at Philippe and I saw that he was trying not to laugh, and of course that set me off, and I got the giggles.

Caro felt her lips tugging at the memory, although it hadn't been that funny at the time. There was nothing worse than trying not to laugh when you knew that you absolutely, defi-nitely mustn't. With the Dowager Blanche's glacial eyes on her, she had had to bite down hard on the inside of her cheeks, and at one point she had been convinced that her eyeballs had been about to pop with the pressure of keeping the giggles in.

Still, I managed a curtsey, which I thought was pretty good under the circumstances but Philippe told me af-terwards I looked as if I was laying an egg.

I wouldn't say your grandmother gave me the warm-est welcome I've ever had. In fact, a midwinter swim in the Antarctic would probably have seemed balmy in comparison, but it was obvious she blamed me for you leaving. Don't worry, I played along and Philippe was bril-liant! He lifted my hand to his lips and kissed my knuckles and told your grandmother that he was in love with me and that he would only stay if he had my support, so he expected me to be treated with respect!!!! He almost had me fooled.

She had better not tell Lotty that her hand had tingled all evening from the impression of his fingers, or that she could still feel the graze of his lips against her knuckles.

I could tell your grandmother didn't like it, but at least she didn't seem to realise it was just an act, so that's something. I had to sit through an icy interrogation about my family, friends, utter lack of connections (or job, come to that), but don't worry, I only gave her my name, rank and serial number. Actually, Lotty, I felt a bit sorry for her. I think that beneath all the guff about duty and responsibility and behaving like a princess, she's really worried about you. Can you get a message to her to say that you're all right at least? Don't say where you are, though, as she's ready to send in the entire Montlucian army to bring you back if necessary! But I think she needs to know you're safe—and I do too!

I suspect the grilling Philippe got was even worse, but it was in French so I didn't understand it. But when our audience was finally at an end we were both very relieved to get out of there. I had to hang on to Philippe as we walked backwards (!!!!!!) across that floor, and he kept hold of me when we were allowed to turn our backs at last and escape. We started off walking sedately through the anterooms, but the further down the corridor we got, the faster we walked, and by the time we reached the staircase we were running and laughing. It was such a relief to be able to let all the giggles out, and somehow it didn't seem so bad knowing that Philippe had had to grit his teeth to get through it too.

Caro paused, remembering how the two of them had run down the grand staircase, laughing. The steps were shallow and carpeted in red, and they swept round and down to the magnificent marble hall where an array of footmen watched impassively.

Philippe had let go of her hand by then, but his eyes had been warm and alight with laughter and that dark, sardonic look had disappeared altogether. Caro's heart had stumbled for a moment when they'd reached the bottom of the stairs and she'd looked into his face. It had been like looking at an entirely different man, one whose brother hadn't died, one whose father didn't blame him.

Shaking the memory away, she went back to her email.

So, I've survived my first encounter with the Dowager Blanche. It wasn't a complete disaster. For some reason her little pug—Apollo?—took a shine to me. He sure is one ugly dog! Difficult to know which end of him is less attractive. I was worried he was about to have a heart attack with all that wheezing, but he came to sit on my foot while your grandmother was lecturing Philippe in French about something, and I made the mistake of patting him. After that, he wouldn't leave me alone. I said I'd take him for a walk sometimes, which Philippe thought was heroic of me, but he was quite cute really, I suppose, and besides, what else am I going to do with myself? Philippe seems to be lined up for royal duties, but there isn't a lot for me to do except sit on the balcony and look at that beautiful lake (which isn't such a bad plan, now I come to think of it.)

It's beautiful here, Lotty. I don't think I'll ever find my way round the palace or get to grips with all the formality, but the setting is magical. Like being in a fairy tale kingdom, where nothing feels quite real.

I'd better stop. Philippe had to go to some reception for financiers, so I've had the evening to myself, and I thought it would be a good chance to drop you a line— or quite a few lines, as it's turned out. It's all so new to me, and there's so much I'd love to talk to you about. Can't wait to catch up properly when all this is over and compare notes!

Hope you're having a fab time out there in reality, Lotty. Let me know, OK?

Lots +++++++++ of love
Caro

When Philippe came back later that night, Caro was already in bed. She was sitting up against the pillows, a book in her hands and a pair of glasses on her nose. Her face was scrubbed, the cloud of chestnut hair tucked behind her ears, and she was buttoned up to the throat in a pair of old-fashioned pyjamas, patterned with sprigged rosebuds so faded they were almost invisible.

No sheer negligees for Caro, Philippe realised. No wispy lace or dainty straps designed to slide seductively over a shoulder. He ought to be glad that she had so little interest in attracting him, so why did the sight of her make him feel so grouchy?

'Don't tell me, they're vintage pyjamas?' he said, loosening his tie and trying to roll the irritation from his shoulders.

'As a matter of fact, I bought them when they were new.'

'What, when you were twelve?'

'I've had them a long time,' she admitted with a defiant look over her glasses. 'They're comfortable.'

'There couldn't be any other reason for wearing them,' said Philippe sardonically. She certainly hadn't bought them with seduction in mind!

So it was annoying to realise how appealing she looked, there in bed. The modest pyjamas only drew attention to her lush curves, and the glow from the bedside lamp picked out golden lights in her hair. Seduction was clearly the last thing on Caro's mind, but she looked warm and soft and inexplicably inviting all the same.

Philippe jerked his tie free from his collar with unnecessary force.

'How was your evening?' Caro asked.

'Tedious. I shook hands, smiled, pretended to listen intelligently to someone droning on about financial forecasts. Welcome to the exciting world of royalty.'

Sitting on the edge of the bed, he tugged off first one shoe, then the other and tossed them aside. 'And that was just one evening! I'm not sure I can stand the thought of another six months of this. I'm going to expire of boredom by the end of the week!'

'Lots of people have to put up with boring jobs,' Caro pointed out as his socks followed the shoes.

'Very true. But give me a night flight through a thunderstorm any day!' Philippe swung his legs up onto the bed and made himself comfortable against the pillows, linking his arms behind his head.

Coming home to someone felt strange. Not as uncomfortable as he'd thought it would be. In fact, he'd even found his steps quickening as he said goodnight to Yan and approached the apartments, and he'd been glad to see the light on in the bedroom and to know that Caro was still awake.

He'd been surprised at how pleased he was to have her

with him that afternoon too. Grimly enduring his great aunt's tongue-lashing, he'd watched her tussling with that stupid dog and felt a smile quivering at the corners of his mouth. Once or twice she had met his eyes with a speaking look, or the tiniest roll of her eyes.

Funny how the Dowager's lecture hadn't seemed nearly so bad when there was someone there to sympathise, to be an ally. To escape with and run laughing down the great palace staircases.

Philippe rolled onto his side to face Caro and propped himself up on one elbow. 'What about you? What have you been doing?'

'I emailed Lotty.' Abandoning the pretence of reading, she put her book on the bedside table and took off her glasses. 'I'd feel better if I knew she was OK. Wherever she is, it's going to be very different from here.'

'She'll be all right. Lotty's tougher than she looks.'

Philippe stretched, yawned and rubbed the back of his head. It felt surprisingly comfortable to be lying here, chatting to Caro at the end of a long day. He'd never done this with a woman before. They'd been lovers, or he'd been leaving. They'd never been friends.

'Did you have anything to eat?' he asked her.

Caro laughed, that husky, faintly suggestive laugh that crisped every nerve and sinew in Philippe's body. 'Have you ever heard that expression involving bears and woods?' she said. 'Of course I did! I felt really lazy ringing the kitchen and asking them to send something up the way you told me. I can't get used to not doing everything myself.

'It's weird with all these servants around,' she said, pulling up her knees and shifting a little so that she could look at Philippe. 'You must have half the population of Montluce working here!'

'Hardly that.' Aware of the swing of her breasts, her

scent, Philippe was horrified to hear that his voice sounded
hoarse.

'They asked me what I wanted to eat, so I said could they
let me try some Montlucian specialities? They sent up these
amazing quenelles of trout from the lake, and the most wonderful tart made with apricots.'

Caro chattered on about food, and Philippe kept his gaze
firmly fixed on her face so that he wouldn't think about how
close she was, or how it might feel to undo the buttons on her
pyjama top very, very slowly, to slide his hands beneath the
soft material, to roll her beneath him and press his lips to her
throat and let them drift lower and lower until she stopped
talking about food and what the head chef said and—

'What?' He sat up, tuning in belatedly. 'You went to the
kitchens?'

'That's what I'm telling you. I took the tray back so that
I could ask the chef for the tart recipe and he was *so* nice.
Jean-Michel…do you know him?'

'No,' said Philippe, who had never been to the kitchens in
his life.

'He wrote it out for me, but it's in French, of course. I might
have to get you to translate it. I can get the gist of it, I think,
but—'

'Caro,' he interrupted her, clutching his hair, 'what were
you doing wandering around in the kitchens? The footman
is supposed to take the tray away.'

'Laurent?' she said knowledgeably. 'He did offer, but I
said I'd rather go myself. I'm glad I did. I had much more fun
down there.'

Philippe pinched the bridge of his nose between thumb
and forefinger. 'It didn't occur to you that it might be inap-
propriate for you to be sloping off to the kitchens and being
on first name terms with the staff? Everyone's watching to
see if you're going to be a suitable princess, and fraternising

with the servants makes it look as if you don't know how to behave.'

'One, there's no question of me being a princess, so it doesn't matter how I behave,' said Caro, 'and two, it's an absurd attitude in any case. This is the twenty-first century.'

'This is also Montluce, which is an absurd place.'

Philippe sat up and began undoing the top buttons of his stiff dress shirt and Caro looked at him sharply.

'What are you doing?'

'What does it look like I'm doing? I'm getting ready for bed.' His voice was muffled as he took hold of his collar and pulled the shirt over his head.

'Aren't you going to use the bathroom?'

Philippe's hands paused at the top of his zip. Caro was sitting straight up, the colour running high in her cheeks. 'You don't need to look,' he said. 'We're stuck with each other for the next few weeks. Don't you think we should at least get used to being comfortable together?'

'There's nothing comfortable about watching you strip off in front of me,' she snapped. 'I bet you don't even have a pair of pyjamas!'

'I can't rival yours for style, I agree, but I've got these.' He waved a pair of dark silk pyjama bottoms at her. 'I've had to get used to wearing them in this damn place. People are wandering in and out the whole time.'

Alarmed, Caro pulled the sheet up to her chin. 'Not in here?'

'Not unless there's a constitutional crisis, but you never know, so don't worry, I'll be decent,' said Philippe. 'But I'll get changed in the bathroom if that makes you feel better.'

When he came out, Caro was lying under the cover, holding it tight under her nose. A pillow was wedged firmly down the middle of the bed.

'I know what you said about having no trouble keeping your hands off me,' she said, seeing his expression. 'It's just to stop me rolling against you in the night by mistake. I think we'll both sleep better having it there.'

Philippe threw back the cover on his side of the bed and got in. 'If you say so,' he said.

To: caro.cartwright@u2.com
From: charlotte@palaisdemontvivennes.net
Subject: Re: I'm here…where are you?

I'm here, and loving it! Thank you so much for being there, Caro. Without you and Philippe, I'm not sure I would ever have had the courage to go. I won't tell you where I am, but it's wild and beautiful, and I've got a job!!! I'm doing all sorts of things I've never done before—peeling potatoes, answering the phone, writing a shopping list, making a pot of tea—and it's fun! I know you'll roll your eyes, but it's exciting for me. By the time I go to bed, though, I'm exhausted, so I'd better be quick. Just so you know that I'm fine, and yes, I've sent a message to Grandmère as well.

I know she can be daunting, but her bark is really worse than her bite. And if Apollo liked you, that will be a big thing. Grandmère might not let on, but she adores that dog. He's her only weakness, so I'm sure she'll be impressed that he's taken to you, as he hates everyone else and is always biting people.

I'm really glad you and Philippe are getting on so well. How well, exactly????? Should I be reading anything between the lines??? Tell me all!

Grosses bises

Lxxxxxxxxxxxxx

Caro was smiling as she read Lotty's message—only Lotty would be excited at peeling potatoes!—but her smile faded when she got to the end. How had Lotty got the idea that there might be anything between her and Philippe? She thought she'd been so careful to make it clear that they were just friends!

Not that there had been much friendliness that morning. Philippe had been crabby from the moment he woke up, and had stomped off to a meeting with the First Minister in a thoroughly bad mood. When Caro had told him she planned to take Apollo for a walk, he'd just grunted at her and told her to stick to the grounds—as if she'd risk taking the Dowager Blanche's dog out into the city. She wasn't *stupid*.

The truth was that Caro was feeling scratchy and out-of-sorts too. She hadn't slept well. How could she be expected to sleep when Philippe was lying next to her half naked?

Yes, he'd had those low-slung pyjama bottoms on, but that had left his chest bare. Solid, brown, tautly muscled, it taunted Caro from the other side of the bed. Her hands had twitched and throbbed with the longing to reach out and touch him, to feel the flex of muscles beneath the smooth skin. She'd tried not to look, but it had been impossible not to notice the powerful shoulders, the fine dark hairs arrowing downwards.

Heart racing, blood pounding, Caro lay and imagined sliding her fingers through those hairs. His body would be hard, solid, *warm*. He was so close, too. It would be so easy to roll over and reach for him.

And that would have been a big mistake.

Thank God for that pillow.

She'd been too hot in her pyjamas, but she didn't want to thrash around in case she woke Philippe. As far as she could tell from her side of the pillow, he was sleeping peacefully, quite unbothered by her presence in the bed with him. She might as well be a *bolster*, Caro decided vengefully.

Eventually irritation had subsided into glumness, swiftly followed by brisk practicality. What did she think? That Philippe would take a look at her in her pyjamas and rip them off her? She *looked* like a bolster, and if she knew what was good for her she would behave like a bolster too.

Otherwise it was going to be a very long two months.

Well, there was no point in sitting around feeling cross. Caro finished the *pain au chocolat* that the palace kitchen had sent up for breakfast along with a perfect cup of coffee—she was going to be the size of a house, if not a palace, by the time she left—and pushed back her chair.

From the kitchen window she could look down at the courtyard at the front of the palace. Outside the railings, tourists milled around, pointing and taking photographs.

She belonged down there with the ordinary people, Caro thought, not up here in a palace, like a Cinderella in reverse, having her breakfast brought up by soft-footed servants. She belonged with an ordinary man, not a prince.

It wouldn't do to forget that.

The *pain au chocolat* had been delicious, but she wanted to make her own breakfast. Philippe was in meetings most of the day, so she could amuse herself. She would go back to the real world where she belonged, Caro decided, washing up her breakfast dishes without thinking in the kitchen. Grabbing her bag, she thrust her feet into comfortable walking sandals and set off for the great sweeping staircase that led down to the palace entrance.

She would go and explore.

CHAPTER SIX

INSTINCT led Caro away from the smart part of town and into the old quarter, with its crooked lanes and balconies strung with washing. Even at that hour of the morning it was warm, but the tall buildings cast the narrow streets into shadow and Caro was content to wander in the shade until she found herself on the edge of the market square, dazzled and blinking at the sudden flood of sunlight.

Settling her sunglasses on her nose, Caro took one look at the stalls selling a spectacular range of local produce and drew a long breath of appreciation. There were glossy aubergines, and artichokes and great piles of onions, stalls selling great hams and salamis or piled high with bread, or enormous wheels of cheese. Her bad mood quite forgotten, Caro drifted along, sniffing peaches, squeezing avocados, tasting tiny bits of cheese and hams that the stallholders passed over for her to try.

Her French was rusty, to say the least, but when it came to food Caro had never had any problems communicating. She pantomimed swooning with pleasure, which seemed so much more appropriate than the only words she knew: *c'est très bon*, which didn't seem at all adequate. It went down well with the stallholder, anyway, who laughed and offered her a different cheese to try.

Before she knew what had happened, she was being plied

with different cheeses and urged to try every one. Everyone was so friendly, Caro thought, delighted. They were all having a very jolly time. She learnt what all the fruit and vegetables were called, and the stallholders or her fellow shoppers corrected her pronunciation with much laughter and nods of encouragement. This was much more fun than sitting in the palace feeling cross about Philippe.

She would get some cheese and bread for lunch, Caro decided, and some of those tomatoes that looked so much more delicious than the perfectly uniform, perfectly red, perfectly tasteless ones they sold in the supermarkets in Ellerby. It was only then that she remembered that she hadn't had an opportunity to change any money yet. All she had was some sterling, which was no help at all when you wanted to buy a few tomatoes.

Caro was in the middle of another pantomime to explain her predicament when the stallholder stopped laughing and stared over her shoulder. At the same time she became aware of a stir in the market behind her and she turned, curious to see what everyone was so interested in.

There, striding towards her between the stalls, was Philippe, and at the sight of him her heart slammed into her throat, blocking off her air and leaving her breathless and light-headed.

Philippe was smiling, but Caro could tell from the tightness of his jaw that he was furious. Behind those designer shades, the silver eyes would be icy. Yan was at his shoulder, expressionless as ever.

The market fell silent, watching Philippe. It was difficult to tell quite what the mood was. Wariness and surprise, Caro thought, as she disentangled her breathing and forced her heart back into place. She could relate to that. It was what she felt too. Not that she had any intention of letting Philippe know that.

'Oh, hello,' she said, determinedly casual. 'What are you doing here?'

'No, that's my question,' snapped Philippe, who was gripped with a quite irrational rage at finding Caro safe.

Lefebvre, the First Minister, had spent the morning droning on about the increased threat from environmental activists who were protesting about some pipeline, although why he was telling him Philippe couldn't imagine. The Dowager Blanche had no doubt already decided what would be done.

He'd found his mind drifting to Caro. He'd been short with her that morning, but it wasn't actually her fault that he hadn't been able to sleep. Philippe couldn't get the image of her in those shabby pyjamas out of his mind. He'd imagined unbuttoning the pyjama top very slowly, slipping his hands beneath it to smooth over silky skin. Imagined hooking his thumbs over the waistband to slide the bottoms down over the warm curve of her hips and down those legs she insisted on hiding away.

This was ridiculous, Philippe had told himself, shifting restlessly. He liked women in silk and sheer, slithery lingerie, nightclothes that were feminine and flirty and fun. He was in a bad way when he was getting turned on by a pair of frumpy pyjamas.

The fact that he needed that damned pillow stuffed between them had left Philippe feeling edgy and irritable and he'd woken in a thoroughly bad mood.

When Lefebvre had finally left, Philippe had gone back to apologise to Caro, only to find the apartments empty. Mademoiselle Cartwright had gone out, the dolt of a butler had informed him when Philippe had established that she wasn't in the gardens either.

'She said that she wanted to explore the city. Mademoiselle Cartwright was charming,' he had added.

Mademoiselle Cartwright was a damned nuisance, Philippe

had corrected him, Lefebvre's warnings running cold through his veins. What if someone had seen Caro strolling out from the palace? She would be an easy target.

Yan had made him stop and work out where Caro was most likely to be. Anywhere there was food, Philippe realised, and they had headed straight for the market. It was that or trawling through every café and restaurant in town.

And now here she was, quite safe and obviously having a wonderful time, and Philippe was perversely furious, with her and with himself, for having, for those few minutes, been so ridiculously worried.

'I thought I told you to stay in the palace grounds?' he said, smiling through clenched teeth. Even though they were talking in English, he couldn't have the row he really wanted in front of all these people, which made him even crosser.

Caro looked taken aback. 'I thought you just meant if I was taking Apollo out.'

'What do I care about the dog? It's you I'm worried about! I told you that there's been unrest recently. I *told* you that's why Yan goes everywhere with me, but you, you toddle off on your own without a thought for security!'

'You also told me the situation wasn't likely to affect me.' Caro actually had the nerve to roll her eyes at him. 'So let me get this right…I'm not allowed to go to the kitchens, and I'm not allowed to go outside the palace either?'

'Welcome to my world,' gritted Philippe, still smiling ferociously. 'Anyone could have got to you without protection.'

'Oh, rubbish,' said Caro. 'Nobody's the slightest bit interested in me. Or at least they weren't until you appeared. If you hadn't come rushing down here, nobody would have had a clue I had anything to do with you at all.'

This was so patently true that Philippe could only grind his teeth and glare at her.

'Anyway, I'm glad you've come, actually,' she went on

breezily. 'I wanted to buy some of this cheese, and I was trying to explain that I didn't have any money.' Completely ignoring Philippe, who was still trying to make her understand the reality of the security situation, she smiled at the stallholder and mimed trying the cheese. He nodded, delighted, and cut off a generous piece, which she handed to Philippe, who was trying to talk about security threats.

'Now, try this,' she said. 'Tell me if that's not the best cheese you've ever tasted!'

Philippe felt the flavour burst on his tongue and he was gripped by a strange heightened awareness, as if all his senses were on full alert. He could smell the bread on a nearby stall, hear the murmurs of the people watching. And then there was Caro, her face bright, head tilted slightly to one side, blue eyes fixed on his face to see what he thought of the cheese.

Cheese! That was all she cared about! *She* wasn't knotted up about the night before. And he shouldn't be either, Philippe reminded himself, irritated. How could he be knotted up about a woman who dressed the way Caro did?

Today's outfit was evidently based on a Fifties theme. Some kind of red top and a turquoise circle skirt with appliquéd tropical fruits. Ye Gods! Only Caro could stand there covered in bananas and pineapples and look so right in them. She ought to look ridiculous, but actually she looked bright and vivid and fresh, and pretty in a quirky way that was just her own.

'Well?' she demanded.

Philippe swallowed the last of the cheese. If she could be relaxed, so could he.

'Very good,' he said, and repeated it in French for the stallholder, who puffed out his substantial chest and beamed.

'Can we buy some? I haven't got any cash.'

'I haven't either,' he had to admit.

They turned as one to look at Yan, who didn't miss a beat,

producing a wallet and handing it over to Philippe without expression while his eyes checked the crowd continuously.

'Thanks,' said Philippe as he flipped it open in search of cash. 'I'll sort it out with you later.'

Caro craned her neck to see inside the wallet. 'Fantastic,' she said. 'How much have we got to spend?'

She was very close, close enough for her hair to tickle his chin, and Philippe could smell her shampoo, something fresh and tangy. Verbena, perhaps, or mint.

They bought the cheese, and then Caro insisted on dragging him onto the next stall, and then the next. She made him taste hams and olives and tarts and grapes, made him translate for her and talk to people, while Yan followed, his eyes ever vigilant.

For Philippe, it all was new. Nobody had ever told him how to behave on a walkabout—the Dowager Blanche and his father were great believers in preserving the mystique of royalty by keeping their distance—but, with Caro by his side, chatting away and laughing as they all corrected her French and made her practise saying the words correctly, it wasn't hard to relax. People seemed surprised but genuinely delighted to see their prince among them, and he found himself warmed by their welcome as he shook hands and promised to pass on their good wishes to his father in hospital.

Montluce had always felt oppressive to Philippe before. He associated the country with rigid protocol and fusty traditions perpetuated for their own sake and not because they meant anything. The country itself was an anomaly, a tiny wedge of hills and lakes that survived largely because of its powerful banking system and the tax haven it offered to the seriously rich. Until now, the people had only ever seemed to Philippe bit part actors in the elaborate costume drama that was Montluce. For the first time, he found himself thinking about them as individuals with everyday concerns, people who shopped and cooked and looked after their families, and looked to *his* family to keep their country secure.

He'd never been to the market before, had never needed to, and suddenly he was in the heart of its noise and chatter, surrounded by colour and scents and tastes. And always there, in the middle of it all, Caro. Caro, alight with enthusiasm, that husky, faintly dirty laugh infecting everyone around her with the need to smile and laugh too.

'What are you planning to do with all this stuff?' he asked, peering into the bag of tomatoes and peppers and red onions and God only knew what else that she handed him.

'I thought I'd make a salad for lunch.'

'The kitchens will send up a salad if that's what you want,' he pointed out, exasperated, but Caro only set her chin stubbornly in the way he was coming to recognise.

'I want to make it myself.'

By the time Philippe finally managed to drag her away from all her new friends at the market, both he and Yan were laden with bags. He hoped the Dowager Blanche didn't get wind of the fact that he'd been seen walking through the streets with handfuls of carrier bags or he would never hear the end of it.

'You know, it would be quicker and easier to order lunch from the kitchens,' he said to Caro as she unloaded the bags in the kitchen.

'That's not the point.' She ran the tomatoes under the tap and rummaged around for a colander. 'I like cooking. Ah, here it is!' She straightened triumphantly, colander in hand. 'I worked in a delicatessen before it went bust, and I loved doing that.

'That's my dream, to have a deli and coffee shop of my own one day,' she confided, her hands busy setting out anchovies and bread and peppers and garlic, while Philippe watched, half fascinated, half frustrated.

'I thought your dream was to belong in Ellerby with the pillar of the community?'

'George.' Caro paused, a head of celery in her hand. 'Funny, I haven't thought about him at all since I've been here…' She shook her head as if to clear George's image from her mind. 'No, not with George,' she said, upending the last bag, 'but with someone else, maybe. The deli would be part of that. I'd know everyone. I'd know how they took their coffee, what cheeses they liked.'

She stopped, evidently reading Philippe's expression. 'At least I've *got* a dream,' she said. 'All *you* want is to avoid getting sucked into a relationship in case some woman asks you to do more than stay five minutes!'

'We don't all have your burning desire for a rut,' said Philippe. 'I've got plenty of dreams. Freedom. Independence. Getting into a plane and flying wherever I want. Seeing you wear clothes bought in this millennium.'

Caro stuck out her tongue at him. 'You can give up on that one,' she said, peering at the high-tech oven. 'I suppose there's no use asking you how this works?'

'I've never been in here before,' he said, but he eased her out of the way and studied the dials. If he could fly a plane, he could turn on an oven, surely?

'Brilliant!' Caro bestowed a grateful smile on him as the grill sprang to life, and Philippe felt that strange light-headed sensation again, as if there wasn't quite enough oxygen in the air. She was very close, and his eyes rested on the sweet curve of her cheek, the intentness of her expression as she adjusted the temperature.

Caro had her sights fixed firmly on her return to England, that was clear. Well, that was fine, Philippe told himself. He had his own plans. As soon as Caro had gone, he would invite Francesca Allen to stay, he decided. Her divorce should have been finalised by then, and they could embark on a discreet affair to see him through the last stultifying months of boredom here in Montluce. Francesca was always elegantly dressed, and she knew the rules. She had a successful career and the last thing she'd want right now would be to settle down. If Philippe had read the signs right, she was looking to enjoy being single again. She'd be perfect.

The trouble was that he couldn't quite remember what Francesca looked like. Beautiful, yes, he remembered that, but nothing specific. He didn't know the exact curve of her mouth, the way he knew Caro's, for instance, or the precise tilt of her lashes. He didn't remember her scent, or the warmth of her skin, or the tiny laughter lines fanning her eyes.

'If you're going to stand around, you might as well help,' said Caro, shoving a couple of ripe tomatoes into his hands. 'Even you can manage to chop up those!'

So Philippe found himself cutting up tomatoes, and then onions and celery, while Caro moved purposefully around the kitchen.

'How did your meeting this morning go?' she asked him as she watched the skins of red and yellow peppers blister under the grill.

'Pointless. Lefebvre is clearly under instruction to tell me everything but stop me from interfering in anything. Apparently, I'm to go out and "meet the people". It's clearly a ruse to get me out of the way so that he and the Dowager Blanche can get on with running things,' said Philippe, pushing the chopped celery into a neat pile with his knife. 'I'm supposed to be getting the country on the government's side about this new gas pipeline they're trying to put in but that's just my token little job.'

Caro turned from the grill. 'What pipeline?'

'It's taking gas from Russia down to southern Europe.' He pulled an onion towards him and turned it in his hand, trying to work out the best way to peel it. 'The easiest and most convenient route is through Montluce, and the government here has been in discussions with the major energy companies across Europe. We—as in my father and the Dowager Blanche—are keen for it to go ahead as it will allegedly bring in money and jobs.'

'So what's the problem?'

'That's what I asked Lefebvre but he was evasive and, when I pressed him, he said that my father had made the decision and did I feel it was important enough to challenge him when he was so sick. So I don't know. People need jobs, and they need energy. On the face of it, the gas line makes sense to me.'

When the salad was ready, Caro tossed it with her hands in a bowl and carried it out to the balcony overlooking the lake. They ate at the table in the shade, and Philippe poured a glass of wine, surprised at how comfortable it felt.

'I forgot to tell you,' he said, leaning over to top up Caro's glass, 'we're dining with the First Minister and his wife tonight.'

Caro sat up in consternation. 'But I thought I wasn't going to any official events!'

'It's not a state occasion.' Philippe didn't think that he would tell her that he had made it clear to Lefebvre that he would like her invited. Even now, Madame Lefebvre would be tearing up her seating plans. He wouldn't be popular.

Caro was looking dubious. 'Will it be very smart?'

'Very,' said Philippe firmly. 'Is it too much to ask you to wear a dress made this century?'

'I can't afford to buy new clothes.'

'*I'll* buy them,' he said, exasperated. 'I don't care what it costs.'

'Absolutely not, said Caro stubbornly. 'I'm not going to do some kind of Cinderella makeover for you! That wasn't part of our deal and, anyway, I don't want any new clothes. I've got a perfectly adequate wardrobe.'

Although that might not be *strictly* true, Caro conceded later as she contemplated the meagre collection of clothes spread out on the bed. She had two evening dresses, one midnight-blue and the other a pale moss colour subtly patterned with a darker green. She was fairly sure Philippe would hate both of them, but Caro thought they were quite elegant.

After a brief eeny-meeny-miny-mo, Caro picked up the moss-green and wriggled into it. It was cut on the bias so that the slippery silk hung beautifully and flattered those pesky curves. She smoothed it over her hips, eyeing her reflection critically. She didn't think she looked too bad.

The dress had a long zip at the back, and she couldn't quite reach the fiddly fastening at the top. Clicking her tongue in exasperation, she braced herself for his reaction and went to find Philippe.

He was waiting on the balcony, watching the lake, with his hands thrust in his pockets. He'd changed earlier into a dinner jacket and black tie, and he looked so devastating that Caro's mouth dried and her nerve failed abruptly. She stopped, overwhelmed by shyness. How could she ever walk into a room and expect anyone to think that she could attract a man like this?

Then he turned and the familiar exasperation swept across his face. 'Good God,' he said. 'Where do you *find* these clothes?'

Perversely, that made Caro feel much better and she stepped out onto the balcony. 'Online, mostly,' she said, 'although there are some wonderful vintage shops around. Do you like it?' she added provocatively.

'I'm not going to say anything.'

Caro laughed. She could cope with Philippe when he was being rude or cross. She could deal with him as a friend. It was only when she let herself think about that lean, hard body that she ran into strife. When she let herself notice the easy way he moved or those startling silver eyes.

The heart-clenching line of his jaw.

His mouth. Oh, God, his *mouth*.

No, she couldn't afford to notice any of it.

Friends, Caro reminded herself. That was what they were.

'Can you do me up?' she asked, glad of the excuse to turn her back to him. She had left her hair loose, and now she piled it on top of her head with her hand so that he could pull the zip up the last half inch and fasten the hook and eye at the nape of her neck.

Philippe didn't move for a moment, but then he took his hands out of his pockets and stepped towards her. His first impression had been exasperation that Caro was wearing yet another frumpy dress, but the closer he got, the less dowdy it seemed. She was standing, quite unconsciously, in a shaft of evening sunlight that made her look as if she had been dipped in gold. It warmed the creamy skin and burnished her hair, turning it to the colour of aged brandy.

He set one hand to the small of her back to hold the base of the zip still, and took hold of the zip with fingers that felt suddenly clumsy. Her neck was arched gracefully forward and he could see the fine, soft hairs at the nape of her neck. She smelt wonderful, with that elusive fragrance that was part spice, part citrus, part something that was just Caro.

Very slowly, *very* slowly, Philippe drew the zip upwards. He saw those tiny hairs on her neck stiffen as his fingers brushed her skin, and he smiled. Caro wasn't quite as indifferent as she pretended. That was good.

On an impulse, he bent and pressed his lips to the curve of her throat where it swept up from her shoulder, and she inhaled sharply.

No, definitely not indifferent.

'Th…thank you,' she managed and would have stepped away, but he put his hands lightly on her hips. Beneath his fingers, the silk shifted and slithered over her skin and every cell in his body seemed to tighten. So small a detail and yet so erotic, he marvelled. It was only an old green dress, it was only Caro, and yet…

And yet…

Philippe wasn't looking forward to the evening ahead. Lefebvre and the other members of the government would go through the motions with him, but their contempt for the Crown Prince's feckless son was thinly veiled. You had to earn respect. Philippe was OK with that, but it would be nice to be given a chance.

But he could forget all that with Caro between his hands. As he turned her, she let her hair fall and put out her own hands to capture his wrists. Her eyes were wide, the deep, dark blue that made him think of the ocean surging out beyond the reef.

'I don't think this is a good idea,' she said.

'What isn't?'

'Whatever you've got in mind.' A flash of the old Caro there, and Philippe smiled.

'I'm tense,' he said. 'I need to relax, and what could be more relaxing than kissing a beautiful woman?'

Faint colour flushed her cheekbones. 'It's just me. You don't need to bother bringing out all the old lines.'

'Maybe it's not a line,' he said. 'Maybe I mean it. Maybe you are beautiful.'

'I'm a friend,' Caro said with difficulty, but her eyes were snared in his and they were darkening with desire, Philippe could tell.

'A beautiful friend,' he agreed.

Dipping his head, he put his mouth to hers, softly at first, but when she parted her lips on a soft sigh, he deepened the kiss, startled by the jolt of lust. His fingers tightened at her hips, but the material just slipped over her skin and he couldn't get a good grip of her.

Almost reluctantly, Caro's hands were sliding up his sleeves to his shoulders, and with something like a groan he gathered her closer. There was a kind of desperation to his kiss as he fisted the dress over her bottom, then let it go in frustration when he realised he was holding silk and not her.

Caro was mumbling 'I'm not…I don't…oh…' but she was kissing him back, warm, generous kisses, and his head reeled with the rightness of it and the sweetness and the hunger.

The ordeal of the dinner ahead forgotten, he eased the zip back down and was backing through the doors and towards the bedroom when a throat was cleared somewhere in the room.

'The car is waiting, *Altesse*.'

Philippe sucked in an unsteady breath as he lifted his head. That was the trouble with having servants. They were always there, ready to remind you that you had somewhere to go, someone to see, something to do. They could never just *leave you alone…*

Squeezing his eyes shut, he fought for control. 'We'll be there in a minute,' he grated.

'*Altesse.*' The door closed softly behind the footman.

Philippe dragged a hand through his hair and looked rue-fully down at Caro, who was flushed and trembling, mouth soft and swollen. 'I'm sorry,' he sighed. 'We're going to have to go.'

Somehow she managed a smile. 'Perhaps it's just as well. I told you it wasn't a good idea,' she added, which sounded more like her.

'I thought it was a very good idea. Didn't you enjoy it?'

Her eyes slid from his and she stepped back, away from him. 'That's not the point. We agreed to be friends.'

'Friends can kiss, can't they?'

'Not like that,' said Caro. 'I don't think we should do it again.'

They were going to have an argument about that, thought Philippe, and it was an argument he was determined to win.

'We'll talk about it later,' he said, taking her arm. 'Right now, we've got to go.'

Dinner was preceded by a drinks reception to which the great and good of Montluce had been invited to meet Philippe. Caro stood beside him, smiling and shaking hands. If she was feeling intimidated by the ferociously smart women whose gazes flickered over her dress, she didn't show it. Amongst all those elegant little black dresses, Caro looked gloriously different.

Philippe was proud of her. She *wasn't* beautiful, but he was having trouble keeping his eyes off her all the same. How was he supposed to concentrate on being a prince when his body was still humming with that kiss? When all he could think about was the creaminess of her skin, her warmth, the delicious softness shot through with excitement? When every time her mouth curled in a smile the blood drained from his head?

And when she was murmuring comments out of the side of her mouth that made him want to laugh and strangle her and carry her off to bed all at the same time?

The Foreign Affairs Minister came up to be presented. 'Look, Apollo's here,' Caro whispered in his ear, and Philippe found himself looking at bulbous brown eyes, a stubby nose and mournful jowls that gave Marc Autan an expression so exactly like his great-aunt's pug that it was all Philippe could do not to burst out laughing. Out of the corner of his eye, he could see Caro biting down hard on the inside of her cheeks. Shaking Monsieur Autan's hand and making small talk with a straight face was one of the hardest things Philippe had ever done.

'Behave yourself,' he said out of the side of his mouth when Monsieur Autan had at last moved on. 'You're going to get me cut out of the succession.'

Still, he missed her at the dinner, which was just as pompous and tedious as he had expected. They sat at a long table so laden with candelabras and silverware that he could only converse with the person on either side of him.

Caro had been put at the other end of the table, no doubt on Dowager Blanche's instructions. Her lack of French didn't seem to be stopping her having a good time. He kept hearing that laugh, the laugh that whispered over his skin and made his blood throb.

Philippe gripped his glass and glared down the table at the men on either side of Caro, who were so clearly enjoying her company. This wasn't the way it was supposed to be at all. He was the jaded one, the one who was always in control. The one who left before things got out of hand. He wasn't the one who sat there and longed desperately for her to notice him.

And then Caro did look up and their eyes met. She didn't smile, and nothing was said, but Philippe looked back at her and the awful pressure in his chest eased at last.

They were silent in the back of the limousine that took them back to the palace. Still silent, not touching, they walked along the quiet corridors and up the double staircase. Only when the last footman had bowed and closed the last door did Caro break the silence.

'I don't think we should do this,' she said as if they were in the middle of a conversation, which perhaps they were. Her voice trembled with nerves. 'I think we should stick to what we agreed.'

'You want to leave the pillow in the middle of the bed?'

'Yes.' She swallowed, knowing that she was doing the right thing but unable to remember why. 'You said you'd wait until I asked,' she reminded him. It was hard to keep her words steady when her throat was tight with desire and the air struggled to reach her lungs. 'You said you wouldn't sleep with me if I didn't want to.'

Philippe reached out and twisted a lock of her hair around his finger almost casually. '*Are* you sure you don't want to?'

'No…yes…I don't know,' she said with a kind of desperation, and he dropped his hand and stood back.

'All right.'

Her heart cracked to see the guarded look back on his face. 'Philippe—'

'It's OK.' He smiled, but it didn't reach his eyes. 'You go and put that pillow in place. I'll be out on the balcony.'

Caro sat on the edge of the bed and looked down at her shaking hands. Who was she trying to kid? Of course she wanted him.

And she could have him, she knew that.

She should be sensible. Philippe was never going to want to settle down and if he did, it wouldn't be with her. There was no point in dreaming about a future with him, but tonight Caro didn't care about the future. She only cared about now, and right then she wasn't sure she could bear to lie there in her pyjamas and know that he was on the other side of that pillow.

The boom and thump of her pulse reminded her of the pounding music as they drove through France towards the border with Montluce. *Let's make the most of being able to behave badly while we can*, Philippe had said as he'd turned up the volume.

Caro's head knew that she ought to behave sensibly, but

her body wanted to behave very badly indeed and, in the end, her body won.

And she couldn't undo the zip on her own.

Philippe was sitting on the balcony, beyond the block of lamplight from the open French windows. His feet were up on the railings, his face in shadow. He had taken off his jacket and tie and the white shirt gleamed against his throat. In silence he watched Caro as she paused in the doorway.

'I can't reach the zip,' she said.

He got slowly to his feet. 'Come here, then.'

Deliberately, Caro stepped out of the rectangle of light into the shadows.

'Turn around.'

She turned and lifted her hair as she had done earlier. Philippe took the zip and eased it slowly downwards.

The night air was cool against her skin. Caro drew an unsteady breath and let her hair fall without turning.

There was a long pause, and then Philippe gently brushed her hair aside to blow softly on the hollow of her neck. Caro shivered, so snarled in longing that she couldn't have moved if she had tried. She was taut, desperate for his touch, and when his arms slid round her to pull her back against him, she nearly wept with relief.

'You know no one's going to interrupt this time, don't you?' he said as he pressed kisses down the side of her throat.

Caro tipped her head to one side and closed her eyes with pleasure. 'Yes.' Her voice was barely a thread.

He cupped her breasts, his long fingers warm through the silk, then slid them lower, burning her bones to liquid, her blood to fire. His mouth was so wickedly exciting, his hands so insistent. Caro leant back into him, helpless against the hungry thud of desire.

'Shall I stop?' Philippe murmured against her ear.

'No,' she whispered. 'Don't stop.'

'I have to wait until you ask me,' he reminded her wickedly, and she could feel his mouth curving on her skin.

An answering smile curled the corners of Caro's mouth. 'Please,' she said. 'Please don't stop. Please make love to me.'

Philippe eased the dress from her shoulders. It fell in a puddle of silk and Caro turned to face him, her skin luminous in the dim light. Putting his hands to her waist, her drew her back against him. 'It will be my pleasure,' he said.

CHAPTER SEVEN

SHE had known it would be a mistake. Her head had known, anyway. Her body still thought it had been a great decision.

Caro lay on her side and looked at Philippe, who was sprawled next to her, his face buried in a pillow. She could hear him breathing, deep and slow. She wanted to lay her hand on his warm flank and feel it rise and fall, wanted to press her lips to the nape of his neck and kiss her way down his spine, vertebra by vertebra, wanted to wrap her arms around him and press into him, to lose herself in his sleek strength.

But then she would wake him, and she couldn't think clearly with those silver eyes on her. Caro tucked her hands under the pillow, out of temptation's way.

She needed to think, to get a grip on herself.

She hadn't known it could be like *that*.

Caro had liked making love with George. She'd liked the intimacy of it, liked the cosiness and the familiarity, liked lying next to him and feeling reassured that he wanted her.

There had been nothing cosy last night with Philippe. It had been harder, fiercer, more urgent. It had been hot and wild, and once slow and sweet. It had been terrifying and thrilling and extraordinary. Every cell in Caro's body was still reeling, drunken with amazed delight.

For her, the night had been a revelation. Philippe had made

her feel sexy exciting, *powerful*. Caro knew that she would never be the same again.

But she was no different from all the other women Philippe had made love to. Caro knew that too. She would be a fool if she thought that she could be. If all those sophisticated beauties hadn't been able to hold Philippe's interest, it was hardly likely that ordinary Caroline Cartwright would be able to, was it?

Her eyes roamed over him, lingering on the curve of his shoulder, the sheen of muscles in his back, the lean lines of hip and thigh. He was all sleekness and leashed power, like a big cat at rest.

How could a girl like her ever hold on to a man like Philippe?

She couldn't.

The pale light of early morning was sneaking through a crack in the curtains. It was time to start being sensible. Caro would have liked to have been the kind of woman who could enjoy a passionate affair without getting emotionally involved, but she had a feeling that it would be a lot harder in practice than in theory.

She was more than half in love with Philippe already, she acknowledged to herself in the half light, with her body humming with satisfaction from his touch. It wasn't surprising. She was only human, after all, and he was gorgeous and intelligent and funny and an incredible lover and a friend. What was not to love?

The fact that he would leave. The fact that he wouldn't, and maybe couldn't, love her in return. And even if Philippe were to think himself in love, it would only ever be on a temporary basis. Nothing in his experience had led him to accept that love could last. Abandoned by his mother, dismissed by his father…it wasn't surprising Philippe didn't believe in happy-ever-afters.

But that was what *she* wanted. Glow fading, Caro rolled onto her back and looked at the ceiling. She did want that happy-ever-after. She wanted to be with a man she could love unreservedly, who would love her back and let her stay and who would always be there for her. A man she could build a life with. A man she could be happy with.

That man would never be Philippe.

If she had any sense, she would tell Philippe it mustn't happen again. She would say that she wanted to go back to being just friends. She would put her pyjamas back on tonight and shove that pillow back down the middle of the bed.

Caro's body rebelled at the thought. How stupid for two single, healthy adults to lie side by side for two months without touching, without exploring the dark, delicious pleasure of making love, without giving into the passion that could burn so high between them. It would be a sinful waste.

Why *not* make the most of these next few weeks? Time enough to be sensible after that, Caro told herself. Here in Montluce, she was living a fairy tale. Living in a palace, with a prince, with a man like Philippe...how could it be real? One of these days, she was going to wake up and discover that she was a frog again, but it wasn't time to go back to the real world just yet.

She would have the next two months, Caro decided. Two months with Philippe, two months to learn about loving and living in the moment. She could allow herself that, surely?

As long as she never forgot that it would only be for those two months. The dream would end and she would go back to the real world, and that meant that she had to be careful. Somehow she would have to find a way of not getting any more involved than she already was. It would be easier for Philippe if she didn't spoil things by getting clingy and needy, and it would be better for her, too, to put up some defences before it was too late.

Beside her, Philippe stirred and rolled over, throwing an arm over her in his sleep and pulling her back into the hard curve of his body. Caro felt the weight of his arm and allowed herself to stroke it up from the wrist, loving its strength and solidity and the silkiness of the fine, flat hairs.

She just hoped it wasn't too late already.

By the time Philippe woke, Caro had showered, was dressed and had herself well under control. She hoped.

Yawning and rubbing his hair, he wandered out onto the balcony where Caro was sitting with her feet up on the railings. For once she looked positively normal, in capri pants and a sleeveless shirt.

In fact, Philippe realised, she looked more than normal. She looked fresh and pretty and glowing, and he smiled, liking the feeling that he was the one who had made her glow like that. He had a feeling that he was glowing himself. Last night had been unexpected. Incredible. Who would have thought it?

'There you are! Good morning…' He put a hand on top of Caro's head and tipped it back so that he could kiss her mouth but, although she smiled, she turned her head at the last moment and his lips touched her cheek instead.

Taken aback by her reaction, Philippe looked down into her face with raised brows. 'What?' he said. 'You didn't mind kissing me last night!'

Caro flushed. 'That was last night. It's morning now.'

'Yes, and it's early morning too. Let's go back to bed.' His hand slid down her hair moved slid beneath it to caress her neck. 'I missed you when I woke up,' he told her, his voice deep and caressing. 'What are you doing out here?'

'Thinking,' said Caro.

'It's too early to think,' said Philippe, but he pulled out a chair to sit down and put his feet up on the railings beside hers. 'What are you thinking about?' he asked after a moment. 'Last night?'

'Yes,' she said. 'And you.'

He slanted a look at her face, hoping to coax a smile. 'I hope you're thinking good things?'

'I'm thinking sensible things,' said Caro firmly. 'I'm not going to pretend last night wasn't fantastic, because it was. You know that. And I hope…well, I'd like to do it again—if you wanted to, of course,' she added quickly.

More relieved than he wanted to admit, Philippe grinned and reached for her hand. 'I think I could bear it. In fact, let's do it again right now!'

'I haven't got to the sensible bit yet.' Caro tugged her hand free with some difficulty. 'In the bedroom, at night, we can do whatever we want, but during the day, I think we should go back to being just friends.'

'What, so I can't kiss you or hold your hand?' Philippe tried for sarcastic but only succeeded in sounding put out. 'What, in God's name, is the point of that?'

'It would help us keep things separate.'

'Separate? What for?' He scowled. 'What are you talking about?'

Caro got up, hugging her arms together the way she did when she was uncertain. 'Philippe, I'm going home in a few weeks,' she said. 'I want to meet someone else then and have a real relationship. I don't want to be hung up on you. Can't you see that if we kiss each other like you wanted to do just now, it'll be so much harder to remember that we're only pretending?'

Philippe's expression hardened. 'I wasn't pretending last night. Were you?'

'We're pretending that we're in love, and we both know that's not going to happen.' Caro turned to look at the lake, picking her words with care. 'I don't want to fall in love with you, Philippe.'

'There's no danger of that, is there? You're always telling me I'm not your type,' he said.

'You're not, but who's to say what madness I'll take into my head if there are more nights like last one and if the nights turn into days? If you're…affectionate…I might forget myself and do something silly.' She mustered a smile as she glanced over her shoulder at him. 'You know how women get ideas in their heads!'

That was true, Philippe thought. Spend two consecutive nights with a woman and suddenly it was all about a 'relationship' and what he wasn't doing right. It was the reason he avoided intimate situations. So why was he getting all grouchy because Caro was suggesting exactly what he wanted?

'I've had my heart broken,' Caro was saying. 'I don't want to go through that again. I'd rather keep things in separate compartments.'

She drew a breath. 'Sometimes…with George…I was trying too hard to be what he wanted. With you, I didn't need to worry about being right for you because I know I'm not, and you're not right for me. I know I'm never going to have a proper relationship with you and it's…liberating, I suppose.'

Unable to meet his eyes, she stared fixedly at his collar-bone. 'But one day I'd like to find someone who *is* right for me and, when I do, I want it to be really special. I don't want to be so hung up on you I can't give myself completely to him.'

Philippe scowled. 'What are you trying to say here, Caro? I'm just a fling before you settle down with Mr Perfect?'

'No…well, sort of, I suppose.' Caro stepped back out of his grasp. 'I just want to enjoy myself,' she said. 'I want to have fun and not feel inhibited, but at the same time I don't want to get so involved that I lose sight of the fact that I'll be going back to Ellerby in a couple of months and then it will all be over.

'No strings, no commitment,' she said, her blue eyes direct. 'Strictly temporary. I'd have thought it would be your dream scenario,' she added with a touch of her old asperity.

It was. Philippe knew that he ought to be delighted.

'We're not going to convince many people of our supposed love affair if I'm not allowed to touch you,' he found himself grumbling.

Caro had thought of that, too. 'Obviously, I'll do whatever's needed to give the right impression, but when we're on our own, well, I'd prefer to keep any intimacy for the bedroom.'

Philippe eyed her almost resentfully. For someone so warm, she could be a very cool customer.

'So I'm to keep my hands to myself until the bedroom door is closed, is that right?'

'I think it would be easier for both of us,' she said. 'You don't want me complicating matters by falling in love with you, do you?'

Of course he didn't. Why would he want that? He'd spent his whole life running away from precisely that situation.

Philippe glared out at the lake.

'You do see that it makes sense, don't you?' said Caro after a moment.

'Oh, yes, yes, I suppose so,' he said irritably.

But it wasn't how he had planned to start the morning.

'Have you seen the papers today?'

The Dowager Blanche picked up a sheaf of newspapers and dropped them back on the table as if she couldn't bear to touch them.

'I haven't had a chance yet,' said Philippe, wishing he were down in the gardens with Caro, who had taken Apollo the pug for a walk.

'Your father gets up at five o'clock every morning to familiarise himself with the news before breakfast.'

Philippe set his teeth. He towered over his great-aunt, but she always made him feel like a grubby schoolboy. 'What are the papers saying?'

For answer, the Dowager Blanche picked up the paper on top of the pile and tossed it across to him. Philippe caught it and turned it round. The front page was dominated by a huge headline: *THE NEXT PRINCESS?* Below was a photo of the market, filling half the page. The camera had caught Caro popping a piece of cheese in his mouth. Her sunglasses were perched on her head and they were both smiling.

It was a good picture of Caro. Her expressive face was alight with laughter and fortunately the head and shoulders shot cut off most of her eccentric outfit. Philippe thought she looked vivid and engaging, and he…he looked *happy*, he realised with something of a shock.

'I could hardly believe my ears when I heard that you had been wandering around the *market*.' The Dowager Blanche's voice was like a lash.

Once she had been a great beauty. You could still see it in her bone structure and her famous elegance, but her expression was one of icy hauteur. She could hardly have been more different from Caro.

'What were you thinking?' she went on. 'We are not one of those populist monarchies, thank God. Your father keeps his distance, and the people are respectful. If you start behaving like the people, you will be treated like one of the people, and you will lose your throne before you have even sat on it!

'This…this *Caroline* is totally unsuitable.' She cast a glance of dislike at the newspapers. 'They're saying you're besotted with her.'

'Perhaps I am,' said Philippe, dropping the paper back onto the table and clasping his hands behind his back once more.

'How can you want her and not Charlotte?' The Dowager's

expression was uncomprehending. 'She's clumsy and badly groomed and she has no idea how to behave.'

'She's warm and friendly,' said Philippe. 'What better way is there to behave? And she may not be classically elegant, but she has her own style. She's...unusual.'

'She looks like a scarecrow,' said the Dowager, unimpressed. 'She's not even beautiful!'

'She is to me,' he found himself saying.

'Then you must be in love! How vulgar.'

Contempt dripped through her voice. Philippe inclined his head in courteous agreement, but inside he felt jarred, as if he had walked smack into a wall.

Love? He didn't do love. Lust, yes, he did that. And that was *all* he felt. He might want to smile at the thought of Caro. He might want to touch her and already be thinking about how he would tell her about this interview. Sometimes meeting her eyes might make him want to laugh, but that wasn't being *in love*.

His great-aunt was watching his expression and her eyes narrowed. 'You can't marry her,' she said.

Philippe turned abruptly and went over to stand by one of the long windows that looked out over the gardens. Below, he could see Caro, who was trying to teach Apollo to run after a stick.

She waggled the stick in front of the pug's nose, and then threw it onto the lawn. Apollo sat on his rump and looked at her blankly. Caro pointed at the stick, then demonstrated by galloping onto the grass to fetch it. She brought it back and dropped it in front of Apollo, who regarded it without interest.

Watching her, Philippe felt some of his frustration ease and the corner of his mouth twitched.

'Why can't I marry her?' he asked.

'I'd have thought it was obvious! You will be Crown Prince

one day,' the Dowager said. 'You owe it to your father to find a suitable bride. We don't want Montluce to become the laughing stock of Europe.'

'Several heirs to thrones around Europe have married commoners,' Philippe pointed out. 'It hasn't done those countries any harm.'

'Those brides at least look the part.' The Dowager joined him at the window. 'Can you say the same of Caroline Cartwright?'

She gestured down at Caro, who had repeated her demonstration with the stick and had stopped to catch her breath. Her face was pink, her shirt creased and her hair tumbled messily to her shoulders.

No, she didn't look like a princess.

Unaware of their gaze, Caro pulled a clip from her pocket and put her hair up in an untidy twist before fixing it into place and smoothing the stray hairs from her face. The shirt strained across her breasts as she lifted her arms, and Philippe felt the sharp stir of desire.

'Everyone likes her,' he told his great-aunt.

'The staff.' She waved a dismissive hand. 'I heard she's been hobnobbing with the footmen and distracting the kitchen staff. Tell her to stop it.'

'It's not just the staff.' Philippe crossed back to pick up the paper she'd shown him earlier. 'The people like her too.' He tapped the article. 'It says so here.'

A lesser woman would have snatched. As it was, there was a definite crispness in the way his great-aunt took the paper from him and reread the enthusiastic piece with an expression of distaste.

'*Everyone was charmed,*' she read, not sounding in the least charmed. 'Hmm.' Her expression grew thoughtful. Philippe could see her clever mind calculating.

'This English girl isn't for you, Philippe,' she said at last.

'You know that yourself. Perhaps you're jaded and she's a fresh taste for a while, but I don't expect it to last and, if you were honest, you'd know that too. As it is, you'll be bored in a month or so and then you'll be ready for someone more sophisticated again.'

And then I'll find Charlotte and bring her home, Philippe could practically hear her thinking.

'In the meantime, if you insist on keeping Mademoiselle Cartwright with you, we might as well capitalise on her popularity. She's new and different, so of course the people are enthused.' She shrugged elegantly. 'Take her with you when you go out on official visits. Perhaps she'll draw some attention away from all these pipeline protests.'

'It might be a better idea to talk to the protestors and settle the issue,' Philippe suggested and his great-aunt stiffened.

'Your father has already made a decision about the pipeline. These people have no business making a fuss about things they know nothing about. Camping on the streets!' She snorted. 'Ridiculous!'

'Perhaps they have legitimate concerns.'

But the Dowager Blanche was having none of it. 'That's not how things are done in Montluce. It is not for you to interfere.'

'One day it *will* be for me to interfere,' he pointed out.

'Fortunately, that day has not yet come,' she flashed back. 'I suggest you stick to what you agreed to do, unless you are hoping to drive your father to his death. He has already suffered enough from your recklessness and irresponsibility.'

She launched into a scathing lecture about his attitude, behaviour and prospects while Philippe gritted his teeth and reminded himself that she was an old lady who had lost both her sons.

'Leave the government to Lefebvre,' she said, winding down at last. 'If you want to make yourself useful, encourage

your more famous—and sober—friends to come to my annual
ball. It's in aid of an international medical charity, so it's a
good cause, and some celebrity guests might lend a certain
cachet to the proceedings. That's something you *can* do.'

Philippe thought about the flights he had funded, the
planes he had flown into disaster areas, the boxes of tools
and tents and water purification tablets that had helped people
survive.

'Certainly, *Altesse.*'

When at last the Dowager let him go, Philippe went straight
down to the garden to find Caro. She was sitting on the steps
from the terrace with Apollo, both of them puffing, in spite
of the fact that Caro had had about ten times as much exercise
as the pug.

Philippe was aware of his tension loosening at the sight
of her. 'It's like a soundtrack to a porn film out here with all
this heavy breathing.'

Caro swung round, her heart lurching unmistakably at the
sight of him, tall and dark and devastating in the suit he had
to wear to meet his great-aunt every day. Every fibre of her
sang and cheered in recognition. This was the man who had
loved her last night, the man whose hands had taken her to
mindless delight. Whose body she had explored, inch by inch.
Whose mouth…

Stop it! Caro told herself fiercely.

It was too early to be thinking like that, but once that bedroom door closed tonight… She shivered in anticipation.

'I'm exhausted,' she said. 'Apollo doesn't seem to have
the least idea of how to be a dog. He doesn't do walking or
running after sticks or anything.' She fondled the dog's ears
all the same. 'Do you, dog?'

Philippe's face was set in grim lines as he sat down on
the steps beside her, hooking two fingers inside his collar to

loosen it. He was looking forbidding, and Caro leaned against his shoulder, bumping it in greeting.

'How did today's ticking off go?' she asked, wanting to see him smile, wanting to see the tension leak from his shoulders.

'Oh, you know. I'm a disappointment to everyone. No sense of duty. Why couldn't I just marry Lotty, blah, blah, blah. The usual.' Philippe spoke lightly, but she sensed it was with an effort.

'Oh, dear, she's not warming to me, is she? After I walked Apollo, too!'

'She's hoping my passion for you will burn out before your wardrobe brings the entire state of Montluce into disrepute. Our little trip to the market didn't go down well,' he told her. 'You're on the front of all the papers.'

Caro sat bolt upright. '*I* am?'

'You're a celebrity now,' said Philippe, 'and now the Dowager Blanche is going to use you. You're to accompany me on the various visits I've got to do. The idea is that everyone will be so excited about what you're wearing that they won't be interested in the gas line protests. She's counting on a media frenzy.'

'A media frenzy? About *me*?' Caro stared at him in disbelief.

'Hard to believe, I know,' he said. 'Especially given your propensity for jumble sale cast-offs. You can start tomorrow. I'm opening a new wing at the hospital in the afternoon, so you can come to that.'

'But won't it look a bit official?' Caro pulled a face. 'Everyone will think we're about to announce our engagement if I start tagging along like that. I wouldn't have thought the Dowager Blanche would have wanted to encourage that idea.'

'She doesn't, but I managed to convince her that I am utterly besotted by you.'

Caro leant so that their shoulders were touching once more. It was amazingly comforting. 'She's still worried about Lotty, and she's fretting about us,' she said. 'Maybe we should tell her that you've no intention of marrying me. That would make it easier for her. You could say you're just obsessed with my body.'

'I could, but I'm not going to. Let her fret,' said Philippe. 'In fact,' he went on, smoothing her hair behind her ear and fixing his eyes on her mouth, 'let her fret right now.'

It was pathetic. The merest graze of his fingers and she went to pieces. Caro swallowed. 'I thought we agreed no touching when we're alone?'

'But we're not alone,' he said. 'My great-aunt is certainly glaring down at us from the window up there, and who knows who else is watching? There'll be some footman who might like to earn a little more by leaking how in love we are to the press. I don't think we should deny him his perk, do you?'

His hand slid underneath her hair and he tugged her gently towards him and, as he put his mouth to hers, Caro closed her eyes at the jolt of wicked pleasure. She ought to push him away, she thought hazily. This was a mistake.

But it didn't feel like a mistake with the sunlight spilling around them on the steps. It felt right, it felt perfect. Parting her lips with a little sigh, she abandoned herself to the sweetness that surged through her, and the current that ran like wildfire under her skin.

One hand rested on the stone step, the other crept up to Philippe's arm and she sank into him, giving back kiss for kiss until Apollo decided that he needed her attention. He started to bark and scrabble at Philippe until they broke reluctantly apart.

'Get out of here, dog,' said Philippe, telling himself to keep it light, not wanting Caro to guess how shaken he was.

'He's defending me,' said Caro, giving Apollo a pat with a hand that was still trembling. 'He thinks you're hurting me.'

'I'm not hurting her, mutt.' Philippe pretended to glare at Apollo and reached for her again, but Caro evaded him and got to her feet, brushing herself down.

'Not yet,' she said under her breath.

To: charlotte@palaisdemontvivennes.net
From: caroline.cartwright@u2.com
Subject: Waving and shaking
Isn't it amazing how quickly you can get used to things? I feel as if I've been living in a palace and hanging out with royalty for ever! It's only been a month, but already I'm an old hand at waving and shaking hands, and my curtsey is coming on a treat.

I'm not sure why, but your grandmother decreed that I should accompany Philippe on official visits—maybe she thinks I'll embarrass him so much he'll dump me in favour of someone more suitable, i.e. you? But you're safe for now. Philippe still can't accept that vintage is a style choice and is invariably rude about what I'm wearing, but otherwise we're getting on fine.

Caro stopped typing. *Getting on fine.* It sounded so bland, but she couldn't tell Lotty the truth. She couldn't tell her how Philippe closed the bedroom door every night and looked at her with that smile that made her blood zing. How they made love with an abandon that made Caro burn just to think about it. How the touch of Philippe's lips or Philippe's hands quivered over her body all day. Sometimes she would look at him and the knowledge of how the muscles in his back flexed at her touch would thrill through her, and she would long for night to come so that she could hold him again.

No, that was between her and Philippe. It was their secret, their other life, the one she struggled to keep separate the moment they stepped through the bedroom door.

Philippe has a punishing schedule, arranged by Lefebvre and your grandmother to keep him out of mischief, he thinks. Over the past month we've visited hospitals, in-spected factories, attended receptions, sat through end-less concerts and admired some really impressive charity projects. I guess you're used to all of this, but it's all new for Philippe as well as for me. I think he's really good at it, actually. He always rolls his eyes when he sees what's on the schedule for the day, but I've noticed that he's got a real knack for seeming charming and interested without losing that glamour that makes people feel special for having the opportunity to meet him in the first place. It's charisma, I suppose.

I tag along in the background. Philippe always tells me I'm going to be bored, and sometimes when I hear what's in store, my heart sinks a bit, but you know what? I always end up enjoying myself. I've been overwhelmed by the welcome we get. I know it's for Philippe, but sometimes people call out to me and want to shake my hand too! Little girls are always thrusting posies at me, and by the time I get home—

Caro broke off. She shouldn't think of the palace as home. It was a place she was staying for a couple of months and she had better not forget it. Ellerby was *home*. She deleted 'home'. She typed instead:

By the time I get back to the palace I'm laden with flowers. My French is improving by leaps and bounds, but I still need Philippe to interpret most of the time. I'm not sure he always translates correctly, because there always seems to be a lot of laughter, and I have a funny feeling it's all at my expense! But he swears blind he's not taking liberties.

So basically, Lotty, I'm having a great time! Even on the most tedious of visits, I can always catch Philippe's eye, which makes it easier to sit through some symphony of squeaky chairs or an earnest explanation of the difference between pre-stressed and reinforced concrete (bet you're sorry you missed that one!) It's hard not to enjoy yourself when everyone is so kind and friendly and nice to you all the time! Maybe I would get sick of it after a while, and I don't need to tell you how sore your hand is at the end of the day after it's been shaken a million times, but for now it's good fun. I've got the rest of my life to be just one in a crowd, after all!

Caro

xx

Not every day was taken up with visits. Sometimes Philippe had meetings with ministers or senior officials and, of course, he had to check in daily with the Dowager. Every morning a red box of government papers would arrive, which he would have to read and discuss with his great-aunt. Caro knew how much he loathed those meetings, and how torn he was between wanting to make some real changes and a reluctance to distress his father.

In spite of the difficult relationship between Philippe and the Dowager Blanche, Caro suspected that he didn't want to hurt her either, so he swallowed his frustration and talked about going back to South America, where he could fly and do something more useful than shake hands. Caro thought it was a shame. He had the potential to be a thoughtful and progressive ruler, if only his family would accept him for how he was.

It was hard now to remember how dismissive she had been about Philippe at first. She had seen him as a two-dimensional figure, a cardboard cut-out of a playboy prince, and he played up to that, as if he didn't want anyone to guess that beneath the glamour and the good looks, beneath that dazzling surface gloss, was a man of integrity and intelligence, who chafed at the restrictions of royal life, while yearning—Caro was sure—for his father's approval?

She fell into the habit of walking Apollo in the gardens whenever Philippe met with the Dowager Blanche so that she could be there for him when he came out. He was always rigid with frustration, and it took a little while to coax him back into good humour, but Caro made him stroll with her by the lake and, between the tranquil water and the mountains and Philippe gradually unwinding beside her, that soon became one of her favourite parts of the day.

By and large, they were sticking to their agreement, although Philippe cheated whenever they were in public. It gave him the perfect excuse to touch Caro: a hand in the small of her back to move her along, an arm around her waist, fingers tucking stray tendrils of hair behind her ears, a knuckle grazing her cheek in a brief caress.

'Just annoying the Dowager Blanche,' said Philippe, holding up his hands innocently whenever Caro tried to protest.

'Stop it,' she would mutter, but she didn't mean it. Ignoring the strict instructions of her brain, her body clamoured for his touch, however brief. She only had to watch him turn his head and smile at the crowd, or bend down to shake an old lady's hand, and Caro's treacherous body would clench with longing for the night to come.

She didn't tell Lotty that either.

CHAPTER EIGHT

To: caro.cartwright@u2.com
From: charlotte@palaisdemontvivennes.net
Subject: Style icon
Caro, you're in Glitz!!!! There was a whole piece about how you've revolutionized fashion in Montluce. I understand a vintage dinner jacket is now the must-have item in every Montlucian woman's wardrobe! I was drinking a cup of tea (I LOVE tea!) when I opened the magazine and nearly spat it everywhere when I saw your picture. Then I couldn't explain what was so funny to Corran and had to make up some lame excuse about thinking that I recognised you. I hardly did! You look like you'd be a fabulous princess. Why didn't we swap places before? Why don't you and Philippe think about making it permanent? It says in Glitz that he adores you…is there anything I need to know?????
Xxx Lotty

To: charlotte@palaisdemontvivennes.net
From: caro.cartwright@u2.com
Subject: Re: Style icon
Who's Corran?????
Cxxxxxxxx

Caro didn't want to lie to Lotty, and it was too complicated to explain the arrangement she and Philippe had made, so she left it at that.

In her inbox at the same time was a message from Stella, who had also seen the *Glitz* article and had made a point of showing it to George and Melanie. George looked sick as a pig, she reported gleefully, and Melanie wasn't looking nearly as perky now.

Caro closed Stella's email without replying immediately. George and Ellerby seemed so distant now. It was hard now to remember how desperately she had loved George, how hurt she had been when he had left her for Melanie.

She was glad that Stella had emailed. It would be too easy to start thinking that this life with Philippe could last for ever, too easy to forget that it was all nothing but an elaborate pretence.

It was time to get a grip on reality again, Caro decided. Already a month had passed. Only another four weeks, and she would be back in Ellerby. Back to where she could find the life she had always wanted: settled, secure, in the heart of a community.

A life without Philippe

She was going to miss him. Caro made herself realise it every day, so that she never forgot that it was going to happen. Because what alternative was there? Philippe wasn't in love with her and, even if he were, she didn't have what it took to be a princess. Her face wasn't right, her clothes weren't right and, however friendly the welcome she'd had at Philippe's side, *she* wasn't right either.

Anyway, she didn't want to be a royal, Caro reminded herself. She would go wild, hanging around with nothing to do but cook the occasional meal. No, she needed to go home and get on with her life. She had been thinking a lot about her deli, and how she could borrow enough money to set it up.

She wanted to stock some of Montluce's specialities. She had learned to make quenelles and the famous *tarte aux abricots* from Jean-Michel, the palace chef, who had given her his secret recipe when he recognised a kindred obsession with flavour. So she concentrated on that, and not on how much would miss laughing in bed with Philippe.

Philippe lay stretched out on one of the sofas and reached down to pull a sheaf of documents from the red box on the floor beside him. 'You wouldn't believe a country this small would generate quite so much paperwork, would you?' he grumbled, flicking through them. 'Report and accounts from the potato growers of Montluce... Waste management solutions for the city of Montvivennes... Forests have been felled to print these reports and who's interested in them? Nobody!'

'The potato farmers might be,' Caro suggested.

'Show me a farmer who wants to read a report!' Philippe looked up at Caro, who was sitting at the table, laptop open in front of her. Her lips were pursed, the fierce brows drawn together. 'What are you doing?'

'Checking my account at right4u.com... Can you believe it? I've only had *one* message in a month, and that's from Mr Sexy so it doesn't count.'

Philippe sat up. 'What are you checking dating sites for?' he demanded, outraged. 'You're with me.'

'Only temporarily,' Caro pointed out, cucumber-cool. 'I wouldn't want to miss out on someone perfect. The good guys get snapped up straight away.'

'You couldn't do any snapping up, anyway,' said Philippe crossly. 'You may only be a temporary girlfriend, but you've still got a good month to go.'

To his annoyance, Caro clicked on a link, and he got up to see what interested her so much. 'I wouldn't arrange to meet him or anything,' she said. 'I could just make contact and see if we've got anything in common. A sort of cyber flirtation. You don't want me to miss out on Mr Right, do you?'

Philippe was standing at her shoulder, glaring at the profiles on the screen. 'Which one is Mr Right?'

'I was wondering about this one.' She pointed at a photograph of someone who had called himself Homebody. He was a serious-looking man who described himself as loyal, trustworthy and affectionate.

Her hair was tumbling down from its clip as usual. He wanted to tidy it up, clip it neatly so that it wasn't so…distracting. Or did he want to pull the clip out completely to let the silky mass tumble to her shoulders? Did he want to push his fingers through it and tilt her face up to his?

Philippe scowled. That wouldn't be *allowed*, or at least not according to Caro's rules. He couldn't believe he had agreed to them. She was supposed to be his girlfriend. He ought to be able to put his hands on her shoulders, or kiss the side of her throat. He ought to be able to cajole her away from that stupid site and over to the sofa so that he could kiss her properly.

But they were outside the bedroom and there was nobody else around, which meant that he wasn't allowed to touch her at all. And he had given his word.

'Affectionate?' he jeered, taking out his bad temper on Homebody instead. 'You might as well get yourself a dog!'

'I think he sounds nice,' said Caro defiantly. She scrolled through Homebody's profile. 'Look, he's a teacher.'

'Why's that a good thing?'

'He'll be sensible, and reliable, and good with kids.'

'Not if he's anything like any of the teachers I ever had!'

She ignored that, and read on. 'He likes eating out and staying in—just like me.'

'Everybody likes eating out sometimes and staying in

sometimes,' said Philippe, determined to dismiss Homebody. 'That doesn't tell you anything.'

'You don't,' said Caro. 'When do you ever have a cosy night in?'

'We've stayed in a couple of evenings.' Philippe had been surprised how much he'd enjoyed both of them, in fact. He'd never done the whole lying-on-a-sofa-watching-a-DVD thing before. With a glass of wine and Caro commenting all the way through it, he had been able to see the appeal, definitely.

'Only because you're here in Montluce. You wouldn't do that normally, would you?'

Philippe couldn't remember what normal was any more. There was only this life, with Caro. Coming home from some tedious meeting and finding her humming in the kitchen. Enduring his great aunt's lectures, knowing that she would be able to make him laugh afterwards. Watching her engage with everyone she met, watching her smile, taking every opportunity to touch her.

Lying in bed with her, talking, laughing, making love.

Waking up with her in the morning.

That was normal now.

Sometimes he would sit on the stool at the counter and watch her moving around the kitchen while he told her about his meetings, and she listened to what he said, unlike the First Minister or the Dowager Blanche. She'd listen and ask questions and challenge him, and Philippe had a horrible feeling he was going to miss all that when she went.

Because she would go. She was always talking about her plans for the delicatessen she wanted to open when she got back to Ellerby. Philippe wanted to tell her to stop it, but how could he? It wasn't as if he wanted her to stay for ever. There was no question of that. He was only here until his father came home, and then he would go back to South America. He could fly when he wanted, party when he wanted. He could date sophisticated women who wouldn't know where the kitchen was. There would be risk and challenge and uncomplicated relationships. That would be much more fun than red boxes and watching Caro cook.

Wouldn't it?

'This Homebody guy sounds catastrophically dull,' he decided. 'You'd be bored witless at the end of one of those cosy nights in.'

'You don't know that,' said Caro, obviously perversely determined to see Homebody as the perfect man for her. 'Look, he says he's got a good sense of humour.'

Philippe was unimpressed. 'Everyone's going to say *that*,' he said. 'He's hardly going to admit that he's dullness personified, is he?'

'We've got lots in common,' Caro insisted. 'He ticks all my boxes: steady, decent, ordinary. A guy like that isn't looking for a glamourpuss or a sex kitten. He wants someone steady and decent and ordinary—like me.'

'I don't know why you persist in thinking of yourself as ordinary,' said Philippe, throwing himself back down onto the sofa.

He felt edgy and restless at the idea of Caro with another man. What if Homebody *was* the one for her? He would be the one coming home to find Caro pottering around in the kitchen. *He* would be able to reach for her in bed and have all that warmth and passion to himself.

Was everything he was showing Caro really going to benefit a man who could describe himself as Homebody?

'Ordinary girls don't dress out of a jumble sale catalogue, for a start,' he said, forgetting that he'd come to appreciate her quirky style. No matter how eccentric the clothes, Caro wore them with flair. Not that he was going to tell her that. It would be no fun if he couldn't give her a hard time about her wardrobe, would it? 'They don't spend their whole time in the kitchen or hobnobbing with the staff.'

As far as Philippe could tell, Caro was on first name terms with every footman and maid in the palace. She knew everyone in the kitchen, and had met all the gardeners on her walks with Apollo. She was always telling him about Yvette's worry about her elderly mother, or the fact that Michel rode a motorbike on his days off, that Gaston grew wonderful tomatoes or that Marie-Madeleine had a crush on the head butler, which no one, including Philippe, could understand.

'Ordinary girls don't have servants to hobnob *with*,' Caro pointed out dryly. 'I'm just being myself.'

'I still don't think you should waste your time on Homebody,' said Philippe, disgruntled. 'He looks shifty to me. What if he's a serial killer?' he asked, raising another objection. 'He's not going to put that in his profile, is he? It could all be a ruse to lure someone ridiculously trusting like you back to his lair.'

Caro rolled her eyes. 'I'd meet him somewhere public at first and, anyway, I've got to do *something* if I want to find someone to have a serious relationship with.'

'I don't know why you're bothering. I wouldn't waste my time on online dating sites.'

'You don't have to. I'm sure the women will all be queuing up to console you the moment I've gone!'

She could at least sound upset at the prospect, thought Philippe darkly. Scowling, he went back to the red box. 'Don't be ridiculous!'

'Is Francesca Allen coming to the Dowager's ball?'

Philippe looked up, eyes narrowing at the apparent non sequitur. 'She's invited, yes. Why?'

'I remember reading in *Glitz* that you and she had a bit of a thing going,' said Caro casually.

'Oh, well, if you read it in a magazine, it must be true!'

'Is it?'

Philippe opened the first file. 'More exploring the pos-
sibilities of a thing,' he found himself admitting. 'She's a
beautiful woman,' he said, to punish Caro for talking about
going home. 'I hope she will come to the ball. It's only a week
or so before you leave, so it would be a good time to catch up
with her again.'

He remembered being bowled over by Francesca's beauty
when he'd met her. Maybe he would be again. Someone like
Francesca Allen would be just what he needed once Caro had
gone. They could amuse each other until he could go back to
South America. Francesca wouldn't be interested for longer
than that, anyway. Yes, she would suit him fine.

'She'd make a good princess,' Caro said in a neutral
voice.

'If I ever think about marrying, I'll bear her in mind,'
he said with a sarcastic look that successfully disguised, he
hoped, the way the thought of her going pressed on his chest
like a small but leaden weight.

Silence fell. Philippe forced his attention back to the con-
tents of the red box. He skimmed through the first two files,
dropping them onto the carpet when he'd finished.

'Now what?' he sighed as he pulled out yet another sheaf
of papers. 'Good grief, a report on integrated weed management! Who writes this stuff?'

He took the first page and made it into a paper plane, which
he sent sailing over to land on Caro's keyboard.

She threw it back. 'That could have a state secret on it. You
should be careful.'

'Yes, I'm sure that intelligence agencies around the world
are in competition to see who can find out how Montluce
manages its weeds!' Philippe flicked through it. 'I don't know
why they think I need to read this stuff, anyway. It's not as
if anyone is interested in my opinion. That weasel Lefebvre

just sneaks round to see the Dowager Blanche and does what she tells him to do.'

The weed management report tossed aside, he picked up the next file and pulled out a piece of paper to make another paper plane.

'Stop that,' said Caro, as it came sailing her way. She batted it aside. 'You won't be able to throw paper planes at Francesca Allen.'

'I'm bored. I hope you're not sending a message to Dullbody—' Philippe broke off in the middle of folding another plane. 'Hang on...'

'What is it?'

Frowning, he smoothed out the page once more. 'This is about the pipeline,' he said slowly.

'The one all the protests are about?'

He nodded as he read on. 'It's an estimate of costs. It looks as if the construction company are lobbying to build the pipeline overground, which would obviously be much cheaper for them. That's a little detail they haven't mentioned to anyone yet!

'What's the betting Lefebvre slipped this in amongst all these boring documents in the hope that I wouldn't notice?' His jaw tightened. 'They've spent a few weeks making sure I'm not expecting anything remotely interesting and now they're banking on the fact that I'll just scrawl my signature without reading this properly. Here, let me have that plane back, will you, Caro?' he said. 'I think I'd better see what that says too.'

Caro retrieved the page from the floor and sent it back to Philippe, who unfolded it carefully and put the report back together. Sitting up, his brows drawn together in concentration, he read it from beginning to end, so absorbed that he barely noticed when Caro got up to make some coffee.

There were footmen waiting outside, but she couldn't get

used to the idea of asking someone to go along to the servants' galley and boil water for her when she had access to a perfectly adequate kitchen to use herself. The Dowager Blanche, she had heard, insisted on a tray of coffee at exactly the same time every day. Everything had to be set out precisely, and woe betide the maid or footman who put the sugar in the wrong place, or piled the biscuits haphazardly on the plate instead of setting them out in a neat circle. Caro had heard that there was a plan of the tray pinned up in the servants' galley but she thought this was probably a myth.

Philippe was looking very grim by the time he had finished reading He gathered the papers together neatly and put them back in the file. 'I think it's time I had a little chat with the Dowager Blanche,' he said.

Philippe was preoccupied as he made his way back to his apartments. The footman—Guillaume?—leapt to open the door, and he nodded absently in thanks.

As the door closed behind him, he looked around, struck by how homely the apartments felt now. It was hard to put a finger on just why they were more welcoming. It could have been something to do with the recipe book face down on the coffee table, the cardigan tossed over the arm of the sofa.

Or maybe it was the smells drifting out from the kitchen. He usually found Caro there, her face intent as she chopped and stirred. For someone so messy, she was extraordinarily calm and organised when she was cooking and she produced mouth-watering delicacies, pâtés and little tarts and savoury pastries which she brought out for him to taste. He would need to start taking some exercise or he'd put on weight, Philippe thought.

She appeared now, wooden spoon in one hand. 'How did you get on with the Dowager?'

'Pretty much as you'd expect.' Philippe yanked at his tie

to loosen it and unbuttoned his collar. There was no question of popping in on his great-aunt. He'd had to wait until the next day, and put on a suit before he could see her. 'I'm not to interfere. Montluce has a delicate relationship with its powerful neighbours, and we can't jeopardise the little influence we have. My father made his wishes known, and I'm to sign the agreement on his behalf and stop asking questions. Et cetera, et cetera, et cetera.'

'What are you going to do now?' asked Caro.

'I don't know.' Philippe paced restlessly, rolling his shoulders in frustration. 'Let's get out of here, for a start,' he decided abruptly.

They drove up into the mountains, Yan shadowing as always in the black SUV. Philippe drove in silence and Caro let him think without interruption. The sun flickered through the trees and the air was heady with the scent of the pines that lined the winding road.

Away from Montvivennes, the roads were quiet and when they dropped at last into a valley and stopped beside a broad, shallow river it was hard to believe that they were only an hour from the bustling city.

'Let's walk for a bit,' said Philippe.

Yan waited with the cars and they followed the riverbank until the water split around a cluster of boulders deposited by a long-vanished glacier, forming deep green pools. It was very quiet, just the sound of the river and an insect droning somewhere. Caro sat on the smooth rock and took off her sandals so that she could dangle her feet in the water.

'It's so peaceful here.' Leaning back on her hands, she drew a deep breath of pine-scented air. Beside her in the dappled sunlight, Philippe had rolled up his trousers and his feet hung next to hers in the clear, clear water. 'I'm glad we came out.'

She glanced at Philippe. 'You've been here before?'

'This was Etienne's favourite place,' he said slowly, looking around as if comparing it to his memories. 'Our father would bring us up here sometimes, until Etienne grew out of splashing around in rock pools.'

He didn't need to add that his father hadn't thought to bring his younger son on his own.

Deep in thought, Philippe looked down at their feet dangling together in the water, and Caro let her gaze rest hungrily on the uncompromising planes and angles of his face. She knew him so well now. She knew exactly how his hair grew at his temples, how the laughter lines fanned his eyes. She knew the texture of his skin and the precise line of his jaw and his mouth...that mouth that made her heart turn over every time she looked at it.

'This is where the pipeline will go.' Philippe lifted his head and looked around at the peaceful scene. 'It's going to rip through this valley, with no effort made to disguise it, and then they'll blast through those hills there, and push it through into the valley beyond. This river will never be the same.'

Caro was dismayed. 'How can they even think about it?'

'There are only a few villages in this valley. Yes, it's beautiful, but what is one valley compared to the energy needs of millions of people? It's not as if Europe is short of beautiful valleys either, they'll say. And who cares about Montluce, anyway?'

'You do,' said Caro, and he turned his head to meet her eyes for a long moment.

'I can refuse to sign the agreement,' he said. 'I can say that the plan is unacceptable as it stands at the moment, and that construction and energy companies are exploiting our need for international support. I can say that the environmental cost is too high. But, if I do, my father will take it as a direct rejection of his authority. He's over his operation, so that's something, but what if the stress affects him the way they say it might? I don't want to be responsible for my father's death as well as my brother's,' he finished bitterly.

'He won't die,' said Caro. 'He's just using his illness to manipulate you, and it's not fair. You can't threaten to collapse every time your will is crossed!'

'You're probably right,' he said after a moment. 'The best case scenario is that he loses his temper with no side effects. I can live with that, but he won't forgive me.'

Behind the matter-of-factness, Caro could sense what a difficult decision it was for Philippe and her heart ached for him. He might say that he was resigned to his family's contempt, but deep down she knew that he yearned for his father to accept him, to approve of him, to forgive him for living when his brother died. It wasn't too much to ask, surely?

Philippe was watching the mountains. 'But it's not just about me and my father, I know that,' he said after a moment. 'I've been thinking about all the people I've met over last few weeks. Decent, ordinary people, who have trusted my family for centuries to do the right thing for the country. Montluce is theirs. They don't want it ripped up and exploited unnecessarily, and if I'm in a position to make sure that doesn't happen, I can't let them down. I can do what's right for them, or for my father, but not both.'

Caro didn't answer immediately. She was trying to find an answer that would make the decision easy for Philippe, but she couldn't do it. 'Your father trusts you to do the right thing, or he'd never have made you regent,' she said gently, but Philippe shook his head.

'He'll never trust me.'

The bleakness in his face made Caro put out a hand without thinking. 'Give him a reason to trust you now,' she said, twining her fingers with his. '*I* trust you.'

Philippe looked down at their linked hands. 'You're touching me,' he said.

'I know.'

'There's no one around to see us.'

A smile trembled on her lips. 'I know.'

He smiled too, then, and leant towards her, and Caro met him halfway for a kiss that made her senses reel with its sweetness. Disentangling their hands, she slid her arms around his neck and pressed into him, and when Philippe kissed her again something unlocked inside her and she abandoned herself to the rush of pleasure. The sunlight poured around them, in them, spilling through Caro, and there was nothing but Philippe, the taste of him and the feel of him and the rightness of being in his arms.

'We'd better go back,' Philippe sighed against her hair a long time later, and Caro didn't resist when he took her hand as they walked back to the car.

Fishing the car key out of his pocket, he held it out to Caro. 'Do you want to drive?'

Caro's mouth dropped open. 'You'd let me drive?'

'If you want to.'

She took the key slowly. 'I thought you'd have to be besotted to let a woman drive your car?'

'Maybe I am,' said Philippe.

There was uproar when Philippe announced that he was refusing permission for the pipeline to go ahead under the existing agreement. The Dowager Blanche was incandescent, and there were worried reports about the Crown Prince's condition from the doctors in Paris. Lefebvre and the Montlucian government quailed before the might of the great energy companies and all those invested in them.

But the people cheered. On the way back from the river, Caro had dropped Philippe at the protestors' camp and he'd walked calmly into the middle of the angry mob. 'I'll listen,' he had said. 'Let's see if we can work something out.'

Dismissing Lefebvre's spluttering objections, Philippe re-negotiated the pipeline deal over the course of a long and bruising session, at the end of which it was agreed that the pipeline would be laid underground, not just in Montluce but along the entire route. Jobs would still be created, energy still supplied, but Philippe had won a package of concessions on the environment that the protestors had put forward.

The public response was astonishing. Philippe's stand made headlines across Europe. *Plucky little Montluce takes on energy giants* trumpeted the headlines. Suddenly everybody wanted to know about the country and visitors poured in, to the delight of the fledgling tourist trade.

Philippe himself missed most of the excitement. He went to Paris to tell his father in person about the agreement he had made on his behalf. 'He may refuse to see me,' he told Caro, 'but I have to try. Will you be all right here on your own for a couple of days?'

'Of course,' she said. 'Don't worry about me. I hope your father's proud of you, Philippe,' she added. 'I am.'

Barely had Philippe left the palace before Caro was summoned to see the Dowager Blanche.

It was soon clear who the Dowager blamed for Philippe's rebellion. Caro had never been subject to the full force of the Dowager's anger before, and she was more daunted than she wanted to admit, but she thought of how often Philippe had endured tongue-lashings from his great-aunt and gritted her teeth. Arguing would only make things worse, she knew, but when the Dowager started on Philippe, she could hold her tongue no longer.

'He is *not* spoilt!' she said furiously. 'How could he be spoilt when nobody in his family apart from his brother has ever given him any attention or credit for anything he does? And he's not selfish, either! A selfish man would have left the father who had ignored him for years to deal with his cancer by himself. Philippe didn't do that. He gave up his life and came back, and he's had nothing but contempt from you and everyone else as a result.'

The Dowager was outraged. 'How dare you speak to me like that?'

'I dare because no one else will speak up for Philippe, and the truth is that he cares for you too much to tell you this himself. But you should look around you, *Altesse*. The people outside the gates don't despise him. They think he's going to be a bold, innovative prince who will take this country into the twenty-first century a decade after the rest of the world. They like him. He's not stuffy or aloof. He's warm and accessible and he listens. He is a good man who's just discovering what he can do with his position.'

'He's gone directly against his father's wishes and my wishes and the wishes of the government in the matter of this pipeline,' said the Dowager, her voice icy with fury.

'He hasn't done it lightly, but he knows it's the right thing to do. Philippe isn't thinking about what's easy for himself, or even what's easy for you. He's thinking about what's right for Montluce.'

'*We* will decide what's right for this country!'

'No,' said Caro. 'The people will decide.'

Philippe returned two days later to a rapturous welcome that moved him more than he wanted to admit. People lined the streets, cheering as the cavalcade from the border swept past and outside the palace, they thronged around the roundabout.

He wished Caro was with him to share it.

She was waiting for him in the apartments, and Philippe's heart contracted at the sight of her smile. The footman closed the door behind him and she threw herself at him with a squeal of excitement. 'You're a hero!' she said as he swung her round. 'Have you seen the papers?'

'Some of them.' Philippe grinned, pleased by her reaction. 'But I wouldn't have been able to do it without you, Caro.'

'Me? I didn't do anything!'

'I wouldn't have had the courage to stick to my guns without you,' he said seriously. 'I'm not sure I would have cared enough.'

'But you care now.' Belatedly, Caro realised that she was still clinging to him and disentangled herself. 'This is your place, Philippe. You can make a difference here.'

'Perhaps.'

He told her about his father, who had been on the point of disinheriting him before it became clear just how popular Philippe's stand had been. 'He bawled me out for not following orders, of course, but in the end he acknowledged that it hadn't been a bad decision. Coming from him, that's high praise!'

'That's good,' said Caro, pleased. Personally, she thought the Crown Prince should have gone down on his knees and thanked Philippe for single-handedly transforming Montluce's standing in the world, but 'not a bad decision' was progress of sorts.

Philippe picked up a book Caro had been reading and made a show of looking at it. 'He asked if I would stay on after he gets back,' he said abruptly, dropping the book back on the table. 'He thinks he'll find it more tiring now, and I could take on some of his duties.'

'What did you say?'

'I said I would as long as I could continue to take some decisions.'

'Well...' Caro's smile seemed forced. 'That's great.'

CHAPTER NINE

THERE was a long pause. Philippe could practically see the excitement draining out of the air.

Caro hugged her arms together. 'This changes things, doesn't it?' she said at last.

'In what way?'

'Well, now you're ready to be here permanently, you really need the right kind of woman by your side,' she said with difficulty. 'Maybe the Dowager was right about that, at least. You should be looking for a princess.'

Philippe stiffened, instinctively resisting the suggestion. 'I don't have to think about that yet.'

'Why wait? There's no point in us pretending much longer if you're going to stay anyway. I'm just a distraction, Philippe,' said Caro. 'It's been fun, but I think it's time I went home.'

A cold feeling settled in the pit of Philippe's belly. 'You said you'd stay two months.'

'That's only a week or so away. I'm ready to go back,' she said. 'I want to be ordinary again.' She smiled brightly at him. 'All of this…it's been amazing, and I'll never forget this time we've spent together, but none of it's been real, has it?'

It had felt real to Philippe. Smoothing his hands over her skin, listening to her breathe, watching her sleep. The taste of her, the smell of her. That had all been real.

Caro moistened her lips as if unnerved by his silence. 'I've had enough of the fairy tale. I'm not what you need, Philippe, and you can't give me what I really want. I need to go home and meet someone I can build a real relationship with. A real life.'

You can't give me what I really want.

Philippe's face was shuttered. It was true. Caro deserved to be loved in a way he never could. She deserved commitment and security and a belief in happy-ever-afters that he just couldn't give her.

'Very well,' he said, his voice tight.

Caro had done exactly what she had promised to do. She had enjoyed herself, but she had never forgotten that it was all a pretence, and now she had had enough of pretending. It had just been *fun* for her.

The cold feeling solidified into a stone lodged deep inside him. He wasn't going to show her how hurt he was. He *wasn't*.

'If that's how you feel,' he said, 'I'll make arrangements for you to fly home tomorrow.'

The Dowager Blanche, however, had other ideas. Before Philippe had a chance to arrange anything, they were both summoned to see her.

'I think she's going to have my head chopped off for insubordination,' said Caro nervously. 'We had a bit of a row last time.'

'You *argued* with the Dowager? You're a brave woman!'

The Dowager looked coldly at Caro when she curtsied before her but, instead of whipping out the blindfold, she gestured them both to the sofa opposite. This was possibly the most uncomfortable piece of furniture Caro had ever sat on. Designed for elaborate hooped skirts, there were no cushions so you had to sit bolt upright, and its gilt legs were so spindly that Caro was afraid the whole thing would collapse when Philippe sat beside her.

There was a frigid silence, broken by Apollo's wheezing as he recognised Caro. He waddled over to wag his bottom at her, and she patted his head.

'Good boy,' she said. He was never going to be the most beautiful dog in the world, and he had steadfastly refused to compromise his dignity by running after a stick, but she was quite fond of him now.

The Dowager was sitting very erect on the facing sofa. 'Well, I see you have been putting Montluce on the map,' she said to Philippe with a true aristocrat's disdain for popularity. 'I was disappointed that you directly disobeyed your father, I admit, but it seems that the decision is not *quite* the disaster we feared it would be. Indeed, your father tells me that you will be staying on to share his duties with him. I am pleased to hear it. You have learnt responsibility, it seems.'

Philippe manufactured a smile and kept his reflections to himself. 'I hope so.'

'I am getting old,' she said, not looking in the least old with her gimlet eyes and rigidly elegant posture. 'Hosting the ball this year will be too much for me. It is time to hand on responsibility to the next generation, so I would like you two to host it on my behalf.'

She ignored the aghast look that Philippe and Caro exchanged. 'Mademoiselle Cartwright tells me that you are much more competent than I give you credit for,' she added to Philippe in her crisp tones. 'I trust that, between you, you can manage a ball without creating the kind of furore we've seen over the last few days?'

'You can't go now,' Philippe muttered to Caro when the Dowager finally let them go. 'I'm not hosting that ball on my own!'

'I've never even *been* to a ball,' objected Caro. 'I haven't got a clue what to do.'

'You just have to stand there and greet people when they

come in. Look as if you're enjoying yourself, and I know you can do that.' He stopped halfway down the great sweeping staircase. 'I know you want to go, Caro,' he said, 'but please stay until after that.'

Caro bit her lip. The ball would be the first time the Dowager had trusted Philippe with anything, and it was an important test. She couldn't leave him to do it on his own, apparently abandoned by his girlfriend only days before.

'All right,' she said. 'I'll stay for the ball, but then I'll go.'

This was one last thing she could do for Philippe. She would stand by his side and help him show the Dowager Blanche what a great prince he could be if given the chance.

And that meant looking the part for once, Caro decided. This was one occasion her vintage clothes just wouldn't do.

There was an extra buzz of excitement about the preparations for the ball that year. Montluce wasn't used to being in the news, and it suddenly found itself at the top of the cool destinations list. Two days before the ball, Philippe's A-list friends began to arrive, exclaiming at the quaintness of the country. The jet set were enchanted to discover that this was one place they couldn't jet to, and that made it all the more charming.

Philippe was torn between pride in his country and a sense of dislocation. These were his friends. He had partied with them, danced with them, skied with them, dined with them... they shouldn't feel like strangers, but they did. Only Jack, fellow black sheep and hellraising companion for many years was the same.

'I like Caro,' he said to Philippe. 'She's not your usual type.'

'No,' said Philippe shortly. He was trying not to think about Caro.

They were having dinner, about twenty of them, and in one

of her mad vintage outfits, Caro was outshone by everyone. She was wearing the same dress she had worn to that dinner with the First Minister, the one she had worn the night they'd first made love, and Philippe's body clenched at the thought of easing that zip down once more.

Beside him, Francesca Allen had an incandescent beauty. She was witty and intelligent and charming, and everything he could want in a princess. He should have been dazzled by her.

But it was Caro who kept catching at the edge of his vision: her smile, the way she waved her hands around, the hair falling out of its clip as usual. She'd said she would be intimidated by his friends, by their confidence and glamour, but Philippe thought she was the most confident of all. She was just herself. Caro didn't have to put on a front because she didn't care. She was going back to Ellerby.

'She's been a refreshing change,' he said to Jack, deliberately careless. 'But she's going home soon. It's been fun,' he said, using Caro's line, 'but it's run its course.'

He shrugged. If Caro was desperate to leave, he wasn't going to beg her to stay. He was a Montvivennes prince, after all, and he had his pride. 'And, let's face it, she's not exactly princess material. I was wondering if Francesca might need consoling after her recent divorce...' Philippe let his voice trail away suggestively.

'Good idea,' said Jack. 'Francesca would put Montluce on the map. She's got that whole Grace Kelly thing going on.' He eyed Francesca critically. 'High maintenance, but worth it if you're in the market for a princess. She'd be perfect, in fact.' His eyes strayed down the table to where Caro was laughing. 'And you won't mind if I chat Caro up then, will you?'

Yes, Philippe *did* mind, but he couldn't say so. He had to watch jealously as Jack manoeuvred himself into a seat next to Caro and set about entertaining her. Jack was all wrong for her, Philippe thought vengefully. He just hoped Caro had the wit to see through him. Jack could be charm itself when he chose.

From the other end of the table, Caro tried not to notice how beautiful Francesca was, or how Philippe rested his arm on the back of her chair, how he smiled at her and leant close to murmur in her ear. There was no point in being jealous. She was the one who'd insisted he'd be good with Francesca, after all.

But it hurt all the same.

Get through the dinner, Caro told herself. Get through the ball. Then she could go home to Ellerby and remember what was really important.

Philippe and his friends were going sailing on the lake the next day. Caro had excused herself, saying vaguely that she had things to do.

It was all very well deciding to ditch her vintage look for something more elegant, but it was so long since she'd bought anything new that Caro didn't know where to start. In the end, she had enlisted the help of Agnès, the most stylish of the maids, who made even the uniform they had to wear look chic. 'I need a dress,' she told Agnès, whose eyes lit up at the challenge of transforming Caro.

Off the peg wouldn't do, Caro gathered. She needed a *real* dress, and Agnès had a cousin whose sister-in-law—or perhaps it was the other way round, Caro got a bit lost in the rapid French—was a Paris-trained designer just striking out on her own.

Ziggi turned out to have bright blue hair, and for a while Caro wondered if she'd made a terrible mistake in putting herself in her hands, but Ziggi made the dress in record time, and when Caro saw herself she was astounded.

'You like?'

'I don't know what to say...' Caro gaped at her reflection.

Somehow those extra pounds had gone, and she looked svelte and stylish.

Agnès beamed. 'You are like a *princesse*!'

'Oh, no,' said Caro involuntarily, backing away from her reflection. She wasn't supposed to be looking like a princess. She was supposed to be looking smart enough not to embarrass Philippe, that was all.

But it was too late now. Ziggi had made the dress for her, and was confidently awaiting a flood of commissions after Caro wore it to the ball.

'It just needs the hair,' said Agnès firmly.

'I'm ready.'

At the sound of Caro's voice, Philippe turned sharply from the window. He'd been pacing around the apartments while she was closeted with one of the maids, getting dressed for the ball. The two of them were starting the evening with a glass of champagne in the Dowager Blanche's apartments, and there would be hell to pay if they were late.

But that wasn't why he was on edge.

It should have been a perfect day. He'd left the red boxes behind and been sailing with his friends. For those few hours, he'd been Philippe again, not a prince. The sun had shone, the company was good. Everyone had had fun. Only he had spent the entire time wondering where Caro was and what she was doing. She'd been evasive when he'd asked her what her plans were. He pictured her at her laptop, planning her return to Ellerby, maybe even arranging to meet Homebody, and he was seized by an irrational fear that she would be gone by the time he got back.

He'd made some excuse to turn the boat back to the palace earlier than planned, only to find the apartment empty. All the wooden-faced footman at the door could tell him was that Caro had gone out with one of the maids and a protection officer. It sounded safe enough, but Philippe couldn't relax until she came back.

Then she'd come in and all the breath had leaked out of him. She'd had her hair cut, and it bounced chic and shiny around her face. The new look flattered the shape of her jaw, Philippe could see that, emphasising her cheekbones and making the navy-blue eyes look huge. She looked slimmer, sexier, infinitely more stylish.

She looked wonderful.

He hated it. He wanted the old Caro back, Caro with the messy hair that irritated him. He wanted to be able to pull the clip from her hair himself and twist his hands in the silky mass. He didn't want this stunning stranger with Caro's eyes and Caro's voice.

'What do you think?' she asked nervously.

Somehow Philippe found his voice. 'I thought you didn't believe in makeovers?'

'The Dowager Blanche is always going on about my hair,' said Caro. 'I thought I'd save myself another lecture.'

She had done it for him, Philippe knew. Now he turned, braced for another new look, and was astounded to find himself hoping against hope that she would be wearing one of her crazy vintage outfits so that he could go back to being exasperated.

He was out of luck. And out of breath.

The last scrap of air in his lungs evaporated at the sight of Caro standing in the doorway. Her dress, cunningly ruched at the bodice to flatter her figure, was red, a rich ruby colour that fell in elegant folds to the floor. Above the striking neckline, her shoulders rose, lush and glowing. She looked stunning.

Philippe cleared his throat. 'You didn't get that at a jumble sale.'

'No.' She moistened her lips. 'I've never worn a dress like this before. Agnès has done my make-up for me, too. I feel…odd.'

'You don't look odd—for once,' Philippe couldn't resist adding.

That sounded more like him. Caro had been feeling stiff and awkward, like a little girl in her mother's shoes. She couldn't interpret the look in Philippe's eyes, but her pulse was thudding and thumping. She was glad to hear the acerbic note in his voice. It made her feel more herself, too, and she relaxed into a smile until Philippe spoiled it by stepping close to her and tilting her chin with one hand.

'You look beautiful,' he said, stroking his thumb along her jaw line, and Caro's smile faded at his expression.

'So do you,' she said unevenly. It was true. He was magnificent in a formal uniform of a dress coat, with gold epaulettes and a sash.

'We're a pair, then,' said Philippe and held out his arm before Caro could reply. 'Shall we go?'

The Dowager's sharp eyes swept over Caro critically as she negotiated a curtsey in her long dress. 'I see you're wearing a decent dress for once,' she said. 'Simple but very effective. Hmm.' Lifting a hand, she summoned her lady-in-waiting. 'Hélène, can you bring me the Hapsburg set?'

Caro glanced at Philippe, who had gone very still. 'What's a set?' she mouthed, but Hélène was already back from the next room and handing the Dowager a flat leather box.

'Ah, yes…' The Dowager Blanche gave a hiss of satisfaction as she lifted out a diamond necklace that made Caro gasp. 'I wore this at my engagement ball. I think it would be appropriate.'

'Oh, no,' stammered Caro. 'I couldn't…'

'Nonsense,' snapped the Dowager, with a return to her old form. 'You'll look naked in a dress like that without any jewellery, and clearly Philippe hasn't bought you anything appropriate. An oversight,' she said, and Caro saw Philippe wince.

'It's far too valuable,' she tried to protest, but the Dowager stopped her with a disdainful look.

'It's just for tonight.' She held out the necklace to Philippe. 'My fingers are stiff. You put it on her.'

'Avec plaisir.'

The diamonds flashed as he draped the necklace around Caro's neck and fastened it with deft fingers. His hands were warm as they lingered on her shoulders.

'Now the earrings.'

Caro put those in herself. She was trembling. It felt all wrong to be wearing these incredible jewels. She wasn't a princess. But the loan of the necklace was a symbol of the Dowager Blanche's approval, another step towards accepting Philippe. How could she possibly say no?

'There.' The Dowager stood back at last. 'You both look most acceptable for once.'

A select group of guests were invited to a formal dinner before the ball. It was served in the state dining room, at a huge table laden with glittering dishes. Caro was relieved to be sitting next to Philippe's friend, Jack, who had twinkling eyes and a merry smile. He oozed charm and flirted as naturally as breathing, but somehow it was impossible to take him seriously.

But then, that was how she had used to think of Philippe, Caro realised.

'Philippe's changed,' said Jack as if reading her mind. 'He's not as restless. Before he'd take off at a moment's notice and the more dangerous the situation, the more he liked it. Just hearing about some of those aid flights made my hair stand on end, I can tell you. It was like he was driven to risk himself as much and as often as he could, and then he'd come back and party, cool as you please.'

He paused at Caro's expression. 'You *do* know about the flights?'

'Yes,' said Caro, 'I know.'

'Thank God for that,' said Jack, relieved. 'He gets very haughty if I mention it sometimes, and just brushes it aside. A lot of celebrities use charity work to raise their own profiles, but Philippe just gets out of his plane and slips away before anyone can thank him.

'I've never spoken to him about it, but a field director for one of the agencies he helps told me once that he finances a lot of the operations he flies too,' Jack confided. 'Of course, the rest of the time he spends amusing himself—skiing, sailing, partying. People think that's all there is to him.'

They both looked up the long table to where Philippe sat, charming Francesca on one side and a haughty countess on the other, and looking every inch the idle aristocrat, as if a thought beyond amusing himself and others had never crossed his mind.

'It's easy to underestimate Philippe,' said Jack.

Caro's eyes rested on Philippe's face, searching for the man she knew was there behind the playboy mask. The man who was teasing and tender, the man who had risked his relationship with his father to do what he thought was right. The man whose smile as he closed the bedroom door made her bones dissolve.

'Yes,' she agreed, 'it is.'

Philippe watched Caro with her head close to Jack's and made himself unclench his fingers from the stem of his glass before he snapped it. They were getting on well.

Too well.

He couldn't blame Jack. Caro was like a flame in that red dress. Warm, vibrant, mesmerising. Philippe was still reeling from the sight of her. Fastening the necklace around her neck, it had been all he could do to stop himself dragging her back to his apartments and kissing her senseless.

You can't give me what I really want.

It hasn't been real.

I want to go home and have a real life.

Philippe repeated Caro's words to himself like a mantra. She was right. He couldn't ask her to live like this all the time. She would hate it. Tonight she might look the part, but this wasn't what Caro really wanted. An ordinary life, she'd said. An ordinary man who would love her and stay with her and be able to give himself completely.

He couldn't be that man. He couldn't let down his father and give up his inheritance to live in Ellerby with Caro. What would he do there? He didn't know how to be ordinary.

And Caro didn't want to be here, although you would never guess it to watch her chatting to the starry guests in the same way that she talked to the staff and the stallholders in the market.

Philippe saw her smile at one of the footmen and hold up a thumb and finger in a message of approval to the chef, Jean-Michel. She had spent much of the previous week in the kitchens, discussing the menu with him. Philippe suspected that, given the choice, Caro would rather be down there in an apron than up here in the state dining room dripping diamonds.

But she knew instinctively how to circulate amongst the guests when the ball opened. Between them, they tried to talk to everybody and make them all feel welcome. The muscles in Philippe's cheeks ached with smiling as he danced with as many women as possible.

Just once did he succumb to temptation and dance with Caro. Holding her close, he thought about how right she felt in his arms. She fitted him perfectly. Her hair was soft against his cheek, and he could breathe in her scent.

When had she become so familiar to him? Her face was

hidden against his throat, but he didn't need to see her to picture the precise bold sweep of her brows, the exact curve of her mouth, the stubborn set of her chin.

How was he going to manage without her? In one blinding moment, Philippe knew that he couldn't.

'Don't go back to Ellerby, Caro.' The words came out in a rush, unbidden. 'Stay here with me. Please.'

Caro pulled back slightly to look up into his face. 'Philippe, I can't,' she said, her eyes anguished. 'I don't belong here.'

'You do! Look at you! There isn't a person here who wouldn't believe you were born a princess.'

She smiled shakily at that. 'This is make-believe. Perhaps I can look the part in this dress and your great-aunt's diamonds, but what about tomorrow when I hand back the necklace and am wearing my vintage clothes again? Nobody would be fooled then.'

'The truth is you don't want to belong.' Philippe couldn't keep the bitterness from his voice.

'I *do*.' Caro's throat was tight. 'I want to belong more than anything, but not here.'

The ball was a huge success, everyone said so, but it felt like a nightmare to Caro. Her face felt rigid with smiling as she moved through a blur of colour and chatter and music. She could feel the weight of the necklace around her neck and she touched it constantly, alarmed by the dazzling glitter of it that kept catching at the corner of her eye. It felt all wrong to be wearing something so magnificent. Caro smiled and smiled and felt wretched. Every now and then she would get a glimpse of Philippe through the crowds, tall and strong, effortlessly the centre of attention, and every time her heart would flip over and land with a sickening thud.

There was a prince who had finally found his place.

There was a man who flew through gunfire and tropical storms if help was needed.

There was Philippe, who held her every night and whose body she knew almost as well as her own.

She loved all of them, but none could give her the home and family she craved.

'I'm never going to belong in a royal palace, Philippe, and you know that as well as I do.' Caro could hear her voice beginning to crack, and she swallowed. 'Please don't say any more. It'll only make it harder than it already is.' She drew a steadying breath. 'I'm leaving tomorrow.'

All around them, people danced and laughed. The chandeliers sparkled and the band swung into a new number to cheers.

'So tonight is our last night?' said Philippe.

Caro's throat was so constricted she could barely speak. 'Yes,' she managed. 'This will be the last time.'

Caro woke first the next morning. She lay with her arm over Philippe, feeling it rise and fall in time with his steady breathing. Her face was pressed into the back of his neck, and she could smell the clean, male scent of his skin. She loved him, and her heart was breaking because she knew she had to leave him. It would be better for him and better for her, she knew that. But it hurt so much, she couldn't breathe.

It had been nearly three in the morning before they were able to leave the ball. Together they had walked in silence, not touching, up the sweeping staircase and along the corridor to Philippe's apartments. Even at that time of the night, there was a footman on duty outside to open the door.

Philippe had barely waited until they were inside before he reached for Caro, and she had gone willingly, fiercely. Late as it was, they had made love in a desperate silence. There were no more words to say.

Philippe stirred and rolled over to face Caro. He smiled at her, and her heart contracted. This was the man she would remember always, the man with blurry eyes and rumpled hair and early morning stubble, not the magnificent prince of the night before.

'We need to talk,' she said, and his smile faded as memory returned.

With a sigh, he rolled back to stare up at the ceiling. 'Now?'

'We ought to decide what we're going to tell everyone.' Caro pulled herself up against the pillows, taking the sheet with her. She had to be matter-of-fact about this. It wouldn't help Philippe if she started howling the way she wanted to.

'We can say that you met Francesca at the ball and we've had a big row because I'm jealous,' she suggested. 'You can tell everyone I've stomped off in a huff, if you like.'

Philippe scowled. 'I don't like. No one would believe it, anyway. You're not the stomping type.'

'All right, if anyone asks, we'll just say that we've decided we're incompatible,' said Caro. 'At least it has the advantage of being true, in a way.'

Philippe fixed his eyes on the ceiling. He had woken to find Caro beside him and, for one wonderful moment, everything had felt right. And then she had reminded him that she was leaving and the rawness was back. This was why he had never let a woman close before. He had known that she would just abandon him in the end, the way his mother had done.

Intellectually, Philippe knew that wasn't fair. Intellectually, he knew that if it ever came to choosing a wife, he needed one who was prepared to let him keep his distance. He knew that Caro would be happy in Ellerby. Oh, yes, intellectually, he knew quite well that she was right about everything.

But it still felt all wrong.

'How are you going to get home?' he asked later, when they were up and dressed and sharing an awkward breakfast.

'I booked a flight from Paris yesterday,' Caro told him. 'I'll get a taxi to take me across the border, and then I can get a train.'

'Don't be ridiculous,' Philippe said irritably. 'Yan will take you to Paris. When do you want to go?'

'When I've said my goodbyes,' she said. She got up to wash her coffee mug and plate, a habit she had never been able to shake. 'I'd better take the necklace and earrings back to the Dowager, too,' she said, determinedly bright. 'At least I can make her happy. That's one person who'll be glad to see me go!'

But her audience with the Dowager Blanche didn't go at all as expected. When Caro explained that she would be going home that day, the Dowager stared at her unnervingly.

'For good?'

Caro stretched her mouth into a wide smile. 'Yes.'

'Why?'

'I thought you'd be pleased,' she said involuntarily.

'I asked you why,' said the Dowager in freezing accents and Caro jumped in spite of herself.

'Philippe and I have decided that our relationship isn't going to work.'

'Nonsense!'

'It's not nonsense!' said Caro, forgetting that she wasn't allowed to argue back.

The Dowager actually harrumphed. Caro had never heard anyone do that before in real life. 'I was under the impression that you loved my great-nephew?'

'I do,' said Caro in a low voice, her momentary amusement fading. 'I love him very much but, as you keep reminding me, he's a prince and I'm just a very ordinary girl. It's been fun, but it's time for him to get serious now and find a serious woman who'll be a worthy princess for Montluce. But that won't be Lotty,' she thought she had better add, just in case the Dowager got her hopes up.

'No,' said the Dowager, to Caro's surprise. 'I see that now. Not that Charlotte appears to be in any hurry to come home from wherever she is,' she added querulously, suddenly no different from any other confused and irritable elderly lady.

'She'll be back,' Caro said, trying to comfort her.

She bent to fondle Apollo's ears, feeling ridiculously choked up at the thought of never seeing him again. 'Be a good dog,' she said. 'Work on the stick chasing.'

Straightening, she faced the Dowager, who was looking haughtier than ever, her lips were pressed together in a very thin, very straight line. But her eyes were suspiciously bright and, on an impulse, Caro leant forward and kissed her cheek. 'Goodbye, *Altesse*,' she said.

There were other goodbyes to say. Down in the kitchens, there was a gloomy atmosphere and every maid and footman wanted to shake her hand and say how sorry they were that she was leaving. Agnès cried a little, and Jean-Michel presented her with a collection of his recipes.

And then came the last, and hardest, goodbye.

CHAPTER TEN

'So, you're really going?' said Philippe. Caro's bag was wait-ing by the door, and she was shrugging on her father's jacket and trying not to cry.

'Yes.' She summoned a smile and squared her shoulders, determined to make it a good farewell. 'This has been one of the best times of my life, Philippe. Thank you for everything, and I...I hope we'll always be friends.'

'I'm going to miss you,' he said as if the words had been wrung out of him.

'I'll miss you too,' said Caro, her voice cracking, and when Philippe opened his arms she went straight into them. He held her very tightly, not speaking, for a long, long moment and Caro's throat was painfully tight. She couldn't have spoken if she had tried.

Eventually, Philippe let out a long breath and let her go. 'Goodbye, Caro,' he said.

'Goodbye.' Eyes blurring with tears, Caro turned for the door, lifted her chin and from somewhere found a smile so that she could leave with her head high.

For the last time, she walked down the sweeping staircase and out past the palace servants who had gathered to wave farewell, keeping her smile in place all the way. Yan was waiting with the black SUV, and he held open the door so that Caro could get into the back. Only then, hidden behind the tinted windows, could she let herself cry at last.

It felt as if she were being torn away like a snail from its shell as Yan drove her back over the hills to the border, and then on the fast road to Paris. When they got to the airport, he drove her right up to the entrance, opened the door and got out her bag for her. She was going to have to get used to opening her own doors from now on, Caro reflected.

She turned to hold out her hand to Yan and thank him. Expecting his usually impassive nod, she was astounded when he shook her hand warmly. 'If there is ever anything I can do for you, *mademoiselle*, you have only to ask,' he said.

It was the first time she had heard him speak.

Caro smiled shakily. 'Just make sure Philippe is safe,' she said.

'I will,' said Yan, and then he got into the car and drove away, back to Montluce, leaving Caro alone outside the terminal building with her tatty bag at her feet, just an ordinary girl once more.

To: caro.cartwright@u2.com
From: charlotte@palaisdemontvivennes.net
Subject: What happened???
Caro, I'm worried. What happened?? I've just rung Grandmère, and she said you'd gone. She's cross with you and cross with Philippe. Then I rang Philippe, and he shut me out. He was talking, but it was like after Etienne died. He was very cool and very polite and somehow not there at all. He just said everything was 'fine', which it obviously isn't. I thought everything was going so well? I thought you and Philippe were friends, but he sounds so distant now, and you're not there. Tell me you're OK, at least.

Lotty xxxxxxxxxxxxxxxxxxxxx

To: charlotte@palaisdemontvivennes.net
From: caro.cartwright@u2.com
Subject: Re: What happened???
Hi, Lotty
Yes, I'm OK. I've been home a couple of weeks, and I'm starting to remember what real life is like. I'm sorry you've been worried, but Philippe is right, things are fine. I suppose you've guessed by now that we were more than friends. I can tell you that now, but we ended it by mutual agreement. Right from the start, we always knew it couldn't last.

Caro stared at the screen. Her eyes were tight with unshed tears and her throat felt as if a great stone had been lodged in it since that awful day she had said goodbye to Philippe. It had been so easy to tell herself that she understood it was temporary and that she was just making the most of their time together. She *had* known it couldn't last, but how did you stop yourself falling in love?

She had tried so hard to keep those nights separate from the time when she and Philippe were just friends, but it hadn't made any difference. Of course she had fallen in love with him. How could she not?

She missed him. She missed her friend. She missed her lover. She missed the way he smiled at her and the way he rolled his eyes whenever he saw what she was wearing. She missed moving around the kitchen, listening to him talk. She missed lying next to him in the early morning, curled into the hard curve of his body.

Caro went back to her email. She owed Lotty the truth now.

When things aren't so painful, I hope Philippe and I can be friends again, but I don't know. I don't know if I could bear to see him with someone else. He's such a special person, he deserves someone perfect. The thing is, I can't talk about him to anyone except you. To everyone else, he's just a prince from some tiny country nobody had ever heard of until the fuss about the pipeline. They can't see beyond the fairy tale to the man he is, and I can't explain. I guess that goes with the territory when you're royal.

I miss Montluce, Lotty. I miss the people and the lake and the mountains. I even miss your grandmother and Apollo! I miss Philippe most of all. Things may be difficult for him at the moment, but he's found his place in Montluce, and that means more to him than he realises right now. When his father comes home, I think Philippe will be able to build a relationship with him at last, and that's what he needs most of all. I don't fit in with Philippe's life now, and he wouldn't fit in with mine, that's for sure, so I know I've made the right decision, even if it hurts right now.

Caro's mouth trembled. Funny how knowing that you'd made the right decision was no comfort at all. Why did everyone pretend that it helped? It didn't. Nothing helped.

Please don't worry about me, Lotty. I'll be fine. I'm thinking of setting up my own deli and café at last, specialising in produce from Montluce, and have even been to the bank to talk about a business loan. That will be exciting when I can get it up and running. Right now I'm temping again, and there's too much time to think, and to remember. Fortunately my 'celebrity status' was very short-lived and limited to those who read Glitz (not that many in Ellerby, thank goodness!) so I haven't had too many people recognise me. My life in Montluce seems so far away now, anyway. It's taken me a little while to adjust to normal life, but I'm nearly there. I know I need to start meeting men, so I've been looking on right4u.com again. To be honest, I can't imagine falling in love with anyone else right now, but I know I have to get back into it. I'm not expecting to meet someone right away, but I can at least show willing.

Caro stopped typing again. It was hard to explain to Lotty the depression that gripped her every time she looked at her potential matches on the site. They were all perfectly decent men, but none of them were Philippe.

I'm glad you've been in contact with the Dowager Blanche, I think she misses you more than she can say.

The way she missed Philippe. But she wasn't supposed to be thinking about Philippe, Caro reminded herself. Hadn't she decided enough was enough? She was tired of this constant ache for him, the constant looking for him and remembering that he wasn't there.

He wasn't there when someone said something ridiculous, or when she turned to catch his eye, knowing that he would share the joke.

He wasn't there to roll his eyes at her clothes or be rude about her cooking.

He wasn't there when she lay wretched at night, longing and longing to be able to turn and reach for him.

Two weeks passed, then three, and it didn't get any easier, whatever Caro told Lotty. She tortured herself imagining Philippe with Francesca Allen. Was Francesca sitting on the balcony with her feet up on the railings beside Philippe's? Was she waving and accepting posies? Did she spend long, sweet nights in Philippe's bed?

The thought of it was a knife twisting inside Caro, and she flinched at the pain of it. The temptation to email Philippe or to look up events in Montluce on the internet was huge, but she wouldn't let herself give in. She couldn't bear to see pictures of Francesca beside him. Knowing would be worse than imagining, Caro decided.

No, she had to get on with her own life. One evening when Stella was out with a new boyfriend, Caro took a deep breath and logged onto right4u.com. Just to look, she told herself. She would never find the perfect man sitting at home. Her mind veered to Philippe, but she yanked it back. She needed Mr Right, not Prince Right.

She hadn't logged on for a while, so she wasn't expecting any messages, but there were two. Mr Sexy was still hopeful, and there was a new message from Ordinary Guy. Well, that sounded promising.

Ignoring the ache in her heart, Caro clicked on his profile. No photo, but that wasn't unusual. He certainly sounded like a perfect match—over ninety per cent. So she ought to be excited, right? This guy was everything she'd ever wanted: steady job, own house, interested in the same things as her. He'd spent a lot of time overseas, he said, but now he wanted to settle down with the right woman. After years of resisting the idea, he was ready for marriage and a family.

He could even punctuate. His message was brief. *You sound like someone I'd like to get to know. What about meeting up for a drink some time?*

So he didn't sound that romantic or glamorous or exciting, but that was fine by Caro. She had done romance and glamour. This time she needed sensible and ordinary.

Stella frowned when she heard that Caro had agreed to meet him. 'Are you sure you're ready for this?'

'No,' said Caro. 'I'm not sure, but I've got to start some time, Stella. I'm not expecting this guy to be the one, but he sounds nice enough. I'm thinking of this as a practice run.'

But it felt as if there was a great weight on her heart as she got ready to go out that night. On the screen, Ordinary Guy was perfect. She should be more excited at the idea of meeting him, Caro knew, but how could she be excited when he wasn't Philippe, when he wouldn't have Philippe's hands and Philippe's mouth and Philippe's body? When he wouldn't click his tongue against his teeth in exasperation, or draw her to him with a smile that promised deliciously sinful pleasure?

How could he do that, when he was just an ordinary man?

Perhaps it was unfair to waste his time, Caro thought guiltily, but she couldn't spend the rest of her life pining for something that could never be. No, she decided. She would go, she would smile and she would be pleasant. She could always come home after one drink.

It was difficult to care what she looked like. Caro rifled through her wardrobe without interest and finally put on the dress she had worn that first night with Philippe when he had taken her to the Star and Garter. She had been wearing this dress the first time he'd kissed her, Caro remembered. How desperate she had been about George then. Perhaps one day she would be able to look back and marvel that she had felt this wretched about Philippe too.

The steps outside the Town Hall were empty when Caro arrived. She looked at her watch. Seven o'clock, as promised. She would wait ten minutes, she decided, and then she would go.

Hugging the light cardigan around her shoulders, Caro sat

on the top step in the last of the evening sun and let herself miss Philippe. Only for five minutes, she promised herself. Five minutes of remembering the taste of him, the feel of his body, the wicked pleasure of his hands. The laughter in his eyes. How easy it was to be with him, how comfortable to lean against his shoulder and feel that everything was all right as long as he was there.

There was a tight prickling behind Caro's eyes and she squeezed them shut, willing the tears away. Just what she needed on a first date: to be caught crying for another man. She shouldn't do this, shouldn't let the bittersweet memories in. It only made things worse.

Oh, God, someone was coming... Caro heard the footsteps and hastily knuckled the tears from under her eyes. Please, please, please don't let this be Ordinary Guy, she prayed.

'Waiting for someone?'

Caro's eyes flew open at the familiar voice. 'Philippe!'

Her heart was hammering high in her throat as she stared at him, longing to believe that he was real, but hardly daring to. He *looked* real. The saturnine features, the lean, powerfully muscled body, his mouth, his hands...yes, they were all as she remembered. Only the anxiety in the silver eyes was unfamiliar.

'What are you doing here?' she asked rudely, too startled to remember her manners or the fact that he was a prince.

'I've got a date,' said Philippe, sitting down beside her on the step.

'A *date*? In *Ellerby*?' Caro couldn't take it in. It was too incredible to have him there, close enough to touch. She wanted to pat him all over to check that he was real. She wanted to burrow into him and press her face into his throat and hold on to him for ever and ever.

'I'm meeting a princess,' he said. 'Who's expecting a frog.'

Understanding dawned through Caro's haze. 'It was *you*?'

'Meet Ordinary Guy,' said His Serene Highness Prince Philippe Xavier Charles de Montvivennes.

Caro couldn't decide whether to laugh or cry. 'You're not ordinary,' she said. 'You're a prince. That whole profile you wrote was one big fib!'

'It said we were a ninety per cent match for each other,' Philippe reminded her. 'And it wasn't a fib. Every word of that profile was true.'

'The steady job?'

'Well, no job's secure for life nowadays,' he conceded, 'but, barring revolution, being prince in Montluce should be safe enough. My father is back in his own apartments, but he's still resting. We've agreed that I'll take over more of his duties on a permanent basis, so I'd call that a job. And I've got somewhere to live, just like I said on the profile.'

'A palace!'

'Hey, it's a roof over my head.' Philippe's smile faded. 'But that's all it is without you, Caro. It isn't a home. It hasn't been since you left that day. That damn palace, stuffed with paintings and antiques and footmen and it's just been…empty. I hate it without you, Caro,' he said. 'Please come back.'

Caro had begun to tremble. 'Philippe…'

'I know what you're going to say,' he interrupted her before she could go on. 'You want an ordinary life, an ordinary man to share it with. I know that. That's why I let you go.'

He still hadn't made any move to touch her, but sat, like her, with his feet drawn up on the step below and his arms resting on his knees. 'I told myself that you were right, that you would only be happy if you came back here, and that I should look around for someone else, who was comfortable with life in a palace.

'I did try, Caro.' Philippe turned his head to look at her and his silver eyes were so warm Caro marvelled that she could ever have thought of them as cold. 'I took Francesca out to dinner, and tried to imagine her as a princess. And I could do it, no problem. She'd make a great princess...but I couldn't imagine her with *me*.

'That's when I realised that under all the trappings, I *am* just an ordinary guy. I'm like everyone else: muddled, insecure, blaming my parents for my own failures. I'm going to stop doing that now, Caro. I'm grown up, and I can make my own choices and live with the consequences.'

He looked away, across the square, squinting a little in the slanting evening sun.

'I've spent so many years afraid to commit myself to anyone in case they left and I had to *feel* something, and then you did leave, and it did hurt, but I survived. If I hadn't known you, hadn't loved you, I wouldn't have been hurting, sure, but I wouldn't have given up that time for anything, Caro.'

Caro found her voice at last. 'You *love* me?'

'Of course I love you.' Philippe sounded almost impatient as he looked back into her eyes. 'I just didn't dare admit it to myself, or to you.' He took Caro's hand at last. 'You must have known.'

'I thought it was just lust.' Caro's pulse was pounding so hard she was sure the steps must be shaking with it.

'There was a lot of lust,' he agreed.

'Or friendship.'

'That too,' said Philippe, lifting her hand to brush a kiss on her knuckles. 'I missed that, Caro. I've never had a friend like you before. I've never had anyone I could just be myself with. I don't think I knew who "myself" was until you kissed me and turned me into a frog.'

He smiled at her. 'You made me realise that I'd been a frog all along. I didn't lie in that profile. Maybe I do live in a palace and maybe I am a prince, but those are just trappings. Underneath, I want the same things all ordinary guys do. I want someone to come home to at the end of the day. Someone I can talk to, laugh with. Someone I can hold and who'll hold me through bad times and the good. That's ordinary, isn't it?'

Caro's heart was so full it was pressing painfully against her ribs and swelling up to block her throat. 'It's…amazing,' she managed while her fingers twined around his as if they had a mind of their own.

'I want *you*, Caro,' said Philippe, his voice deep and urgent. 'Not just someone. You. I need you there, with me.'

'But what about your father? He'll be so angry. And the Dowager Blanche…they won't let you be ordinary, Philippe.' Caro was struggling to be sensible. In her head, she had been through this so many times. 'It's incredible that you love me,' she made herself say, 'but it doesn't change who I am, and it doesn't change who you are. You're still a prince and I'm never going to make a princess.'

Tenderly, Philippe pushed a curl back from her face. 'You're the only one who thinks so.'

'The Dowager Blanche certainly doesn't think so!'

'Oh, yes, she does. She might not show it, but she likes you. She liked the way you stood up to her. Apollo might have put in a good word too, because she told me that I was a great dolt for letting you go.'

Caro's jaw dropped. *'Really?'*

'Really,' said Philippe with a smile. 'The Montlucians think you'd make a great princess, too. There's an entire country waiting for you to come back, Caro! As for my father, he's just pleased that I'm ready to settle down. Even Yan opened his mouth and wished me luck.'

Caro shook her head to clear her spinning mind, but Philippe misinterpreted the gesture. 'Don't say no!' he said, grabbing her other hand and pulling her round to face him. 'I know how you've always dreamed of an ordinary life, Caro, but why settle for ordinary when what we've got could be *extraordinary*?

'And I don't mean where and how we live,' he went on with an edge of desperation. 'I mean being together, being friends, loving each other and trusting each other and being there for each other. We're so lucky to have found someone we can have that with. *That's* what's extraordinary.'

Caro stared at him. Philippe was right. Was she holding onto one dream because she was scared to reach for a bigger and better one?

'Ordinary Guy sounded so perfect,' she said slowly. 'Exactly the man I'd always wanted.'

'He is perfect,' said Philippe. 'I made damn sure he would be when I wrote that profile. I didn't want to risk you not agreeing to meet me.'

'I still don't understand why you didn't just ring. It would have been much easier.'

'But then you'd have just come out with all that you're-a-prince-I'm-unsuitable stuff and refused to meet me,' he pointed out. 'It was the only way I could think of to talk to you and make you see me not as a prince, but as the ordinary guy you've wanted all along.'

Caro pulled her hand from his to lay her palm against his cheek. 'You did it very well,' she told him. 'I was convinced that I would never find anyone more suitable for me, and yet when I walked down here I was more depressed than I've ever been in my life.'

'*Depressed?*'

A smile trembled on her lips. 'Because I knew that however perfect Ordinary Guy was on paper, I'd already met the perfect man for me, and he wasn't ordinary at all.'

Philippe let out a long breath. 'He wouldn't happen to be a prince, would he?' he asked hopefully, turning his face so that he could press a kiss into her palm.

'He would,' said Caro. 'When you came just now, I was crying. I'd just realised that even though he was nothing like the kind of man I thought I wanted, only he would do.' The blue eyes filled with tears. 'And now you're here, and I'm so happy, I can't believe it...' Her voice broke.

'Caro.' Philippe reached for her then, pushing his hands into her hair and pulling her into him for a long, long, sweet kiss. 'Caro, say you love me,' he mumbled against her temple when he lifted his head at last.

'I love you...I love you...I do,' she stammered, incoherent with happiness.

'Say you'll marry me and be my princess.'

She stilled at that, knowing that this was her last chance to grasp at being sensible. Placing the flat of her hands against his chest, she held herself away from him. 'Are you sure, Philippe?' she said doubtfully. 'I do love you, but we're so different. It won't be easy.'

'No, it won't be,' said Philippe. 'But who wants easy when they can have incredible? Yes, we'll have to work through some tough bits, but won't that be worth it when we see what an amazing life we can build together?'

He drew her back against him. 'Come on, Caro, stop looking for difficulties. Just kiss me again and tell me you'll marry me.'

Caro's eyes were starry with happiness as she wound her arms around his neck. 'All right,' she said obediently. 'I will.'

'Ready?' Lotty smiled as she twitched Caro's train into place. 'How do you feel?'

'I can't believe this is really happening,' Caro confessed. Outside, she could hear the church bells ringing across the wintry city in great, joyous peals. 'I keep thinking I must be dreaming.'

'Then I'm in the same dream,' said Stella, peeking out of the window. 'Have you *seen* how many people there are out there? The entire population of Montluce has come to see you married, Caro!'

'No pressure, then!'

'You'll be fine,' Lotty soothed. 'And you look incredible.'

'Thanks to your grandmother.' Caro smoothed down her dress with unsteady hands. Soon after she'd returned to Montluce, the Dowager had taken her aside and stiffly offered her the dress that she had worn for her own wedding fifty-five years earlier.

'I've observed that you don't wear new clothes,' she had said. 'But of course, if you would prefer a new designer dress, that is entirely up to you.'

But Caro had been thrilled with the dress. It was a dress fit for a princess, with full skirts, a fitted bodice and a spectacular train. Lace covered her arms and the ivory satin was sewn with seed pearls that gleamed and shimmered as she moved. It had had to be let out in places, that was true, but it felt very special to be getting married in the Dowager's dress. Lotty's grandmother had lent her diamond drop earrings, too, and the antique corsage tiara that held the gossamer fine veil in place.

Now it was time to go. Caro was shaking with nerves as she lifted her skirts to walk carefully down the great staircase. Philippe's father was waiting for her at the bottom. He was an austere man, still thin from his treatment, but growing stronger every day. Caro had been pleased to see the wary relationship that was growing between father and son. As she had no father and no close male relatives, the Crown Prince had offered to give her away himself, and now he smiled at the sight of her.

'My son is a lucky man,' he said. 'Come, let us go.'

A big, low limousine with wide windows waited in the courtyard, where what seemed like the entire palace staff had turned out to wish her well for her wedding. They cheered as Caro was helped into the car by a footman, and the train was piled in after her. Then Philippe's father got in beside her.

As the car came out of the gates, another huge cheer went up from the waiting crowds. The flag at the front of the car fluttered as they drove along streets lined with smiling, waving people and the frosty air rang with bells. Caro's throat thickened with nervousness and emotion and she gripped the bouquet of white roses so tightly her knuckles showed white.

A feeling of unreality had her in its grip, and her smile felt as if it had been fixed on her face. This couldn't be real. This couldn't be her, Caro Cartwright, being driven through cheering crowds to marry a prince. Any minute now, she would wake up and find that she had been dreaming.

Then they were at the cathedral, and Lotty and Stella were there to help her out of the car and pull out the train onto the red carpet. The cheers were even louder there. Caro's smile felt more wooden than ever. She wasn't nervous, she realised. She was terrified.

The Crown Prince offered his arm. As they entered the cathedral, the big wooden doors swung shut behind them and the trumpeters in the clerestory struck up.

Caro had an impression of a mass of people, all smiling, all staring at her. She could feel the train dragging behind her, the weight of the tiara on her head, the heavy satin skirts. The aisle seemed to go on for ever, while the music swelled. It had to be a dream.

And then she saw Philippe waiting at the altar. He was dressed in full regalia, with golden epaulettes, medals and a sash across his chest and a sword at his side, but Caro didn't see the uniform. She saw the smile that was just for her and, all at once, the dreamlike feeling vanished, and she forgot the television cameras and the watching congregation. There was just Philippe, waiting for her, and it was real after all.

Theirs might be an extraordinary wedding, but the vows they were making were the same that every couple made, and they were real too.

When it was over, Philippe kissed her there in front of everybody, and they made their way back down the aisle. The bells were pealing and the sun glittered on the snowy rooftops as they emerged from the cathedral to cheers and whistles.

A carriage drawn by six white horses with nodding plumes waited at the bottom of the steps. Philippe and Caro smiled and waved, and then the train had to be negotiated into another vehicle, but at last they were in and they set off through the city streets lined with crowds. Caro's arm was already aching from all the waving.

'You've still got the balcony to go,' murmured Philippe, 'but let's give them something else to cheer about.' And he kissed her thoroughly, to the delight of the cheering, flag-waving crowd.

Caro was flushed and laughing when they got back to the palace. They paused for a moment to wave to the crowds once more before stepping into the cool of the marbled hall out of sight of the cameras. Even then there was no opportunity to be alone. The hall was lined with palace servants, and Caro had her first taste of how her life had changed when she was greeted with smiling bows and curtseys. Laughing, she hooked her train over her arm, and together she and Philippe climbed the staircase she had descended so nervously earlier.

The reception was to be held in the state ballroom. 'Quick,' said Philippe, opening a door to one of the side rooms. 'Before the others get here!' And he pulled Caro inside and kissed her against the door until they heard the unmistakable sounds of everyone else arriving.

'I suppose we can't skip out on our own wedding,' he said regretfully, letting her go at last.

'Careful of the Dowager's dress!' Blushing, Caro patted her hair and wondered if it was going to be obvious to everyone what they'd been doing. She hadn't put up much of a protest. 'Now I need to redo my make-up. Agnès will kill me!'

'She can't be cross with you now. You're a princess,' said Philippe. 'Besides, you look beautiful.' He studied her critically for a moment before straightening her tiara. 'There, you're ready to go again.'

He stayed by her side as they moved through the throng of guests. Caro smiled and kissed endless cheeks, but all the time she was acutely aware of Philippe, of his touch on her back, his hand on hers, his arm at her waist.

Outside, she was vaguely aware of chanting, but it was only when the doors were thrown open and she and Philippe stepped out onto the balcony to a roar of approval that Caro realised how many people were gathered outside waiting to see them. The sheer number and noise of the crowd made her gasp.

The view down over the mass of fluttering Montluce flags was dizzying.

'Philippe,' she said, turning to him with her heart in her eyes. 'I've just had a revelation.'

'I hope that it's how much you love me?' said Philippe, waving at the crowds.

Caro slid her hand into his. 'All those years I longed for a place to belong, and I never dreamt I would feel that I did on a palace balcony! But it isn't about a place,' she realised wonderingly. 'It's about being with you.'

'Quite right.' Philippe grinned and pulled her into him for a kiss while the crowd roared and cheered and whistled and waved flags below. '*This* is where you belong, Caro. Right here in my arms.'

'I've found my frog at last,' she sighed happily.

Philippe watched her turn to wave and smile at her new subjects, and he held her hand tight in his. 'And I've found my princess,' he said.

JUNE 2011
HARDBACK TITLES

ROMANCE

Passion and the Prince	Penny Jordan
For Duty's Sake	Lucy Monroe
Alessandro's Prize	Helen Bianchin
Mr and Mischief	Kate Hewitt
Wife in the Shadows	Sara Craven
The Brooding Stranger	Maggie Cox
An Inconvenient Obsession	Natasha Tate
The Girl He Never Noticed	Lindsay Armstrong
The Privileged and the Damned	Kimberly Lang
The Big Bad Boss	Susan Stephens
Her Desert Prince	Rebecca Winters
A Family for the Rugged Rancher	Donna Alward
The Boss's Surprise Son	Teresa Carpenter
Soldier on Her Doorstep	Soraya Lane
Ordinary Girl in a Tiara	Jessica Hart
Tempted by Trouble	Liz Fielding
Flirting with the Society Doctor	Janice Lynn
When One Night Isn't Enough	Wendy S Marcus

HISTORICAL

Ravished by the Rake	Louise Allen
The Rake of Hollowhurst Castle	Elizabeth Beacon
Bought for the Harem	Anne Herries
Slave Princess	Juliet Landon

MEDICAL™

Melting the Argentine Doctor's Heart	Meredith Webber
Small Town Marriage Miracle	Jennifer Taylor
St Piran's: Prince on the Children's Ward	Sarah Morgan
Harry St Clair: Rogue or Doctor?	Fiona McArthur

05011 Gen Std LP

 JUNE 2011 LARGE PRINT TITLES

ROMANCE

HISTORICAL

MEDICAL™

JULY 2011
HARDBACK TITLES

ROMANCE

The Marriage Betrayal	Lynne Graham
The Ice Prince	Sandra Marton
Doukakis's Apprentice	Sarah Morgan
Surrender to the Past	Carole Mortimer
Heart of the Desert	Carol Marinelli
Reckless Night in Rio	Jennie Lucas
Her Impossible Boss	Cathy Williams
The Replacement Wife	Caitlin Crews
Dating and Other Dangers	Natalie Anderson
The S Before Ex	Mira Lyn Kelly
Her Outback Commander	Margaret Way
A Kiss to Seal the Deal	Nikki Logan
Baby on the Ranch	Susan Meier
The Army Ranger's Return	Soraya Lane
Girl in a Vintage Dress	Nicola Marsh
Rapunzel in New York	Nikki Logan
The Doctor & the Runaway Heiress	Marion Lennox
The Surgeon She Never Forgot	Melanie Milburne

HISTORICAL

Seduced by the Scoundrel	Louise Allen
Unmasking the Duke's Mistress	Margaret McPhee
To Catch a Husband…	Sarah Mallory
The Highlander's Redemption	Marguerite Kaye

MEDICAL™

The Playboy of Harley Street	Anne Fraser
Doctor on the Red Carpet	Anne Fraser
Just One Last Night…	Amy Andrews
Suddenly Single Sophie	Leonie Knight

JULY 2011
LARGE PRINT TITLES

ROMANCE

A Stormy Spanish Summer	Penny Jordan
Taming the Last St Claire	Carole Mortimer
Not a Marrying Man	Miranda Lee
The Far Side of Paradise	Robyn Donald
The Baby Swap Miracle	Caroline Anderson
Expecting Royal Twins!	Melissa McClone
To Dance with a Prince	Cara Colter
Molly Cooper's Dream Date	Barbara Hannay

HISTORICAL

Lady Folbroke's Delicious Deception	Christine Merrill
Breaking the Governess's Rules	Michelle Styles
Her Dark and Dangerous Lord	Anne Herries
How To Marry a Rake	Deb Marlowe

MEDICAL™

Sheikh, Children's Doctor...Husband	Meredith Webber
Six-Week Marriage Miracle	Jessica Matthews
Rescued by the Dreamy Doc	Amy Andrews
Navy Officer to Family Man	Emily Forbes
St Piran's: Italian Surgeon, Forbidden Bride	Margaret McDonagh
The Baby Who Stole the Doctor's Heart	Dianne Drake